The Scarlet Petal
and other stories

The Scarlet Petal

and other stories

by

Ryan Petrie

Illustrated by

Aidan Donald

evertype

2021

Published by Evertype, 19A Corso Street, Dundee, DD2 1DR, Scotland.
www.evertype.com.

First edition 2021.

A catalogue record for this book is available from the British Library.

ISBN-10 1-78201-262-1
ISBN-13 978-1-78201-262-7

Set in Minion Pro and Étienne by Michael Everson.

Cover: Michael Everson.

Contents

*This book is dedicated with love and affection
to my friends and family,
who kindly encouraged my talents as a writer,
whatever they might be.*

*I also make room in this dedication for the people
who I wish could be here but are not:
to my grandparents, John, James, and Joyce.*

*In memory of my dear friend Michael Walker,
who loved fairy tales very much.*

Foreword:
Putting pen to paper

It takes a lot of courage to put pen to paper, more courage than I here possess. And that is what I love doing most: scratching symbols onto paper, and making a world emerge from them.

I love the act of putting one word after another, of taking myself and whoever might read these words on a journey to discover the things we might not have known at first, but will know intimately when the journey comes to an end. I love that feeling, and I wonder whether or not I will ever stop loving it. I hope I not, even if it means things won't get done. Sometimes I want to have a piece of work I am writing all to myself and never finish it—but I know now that defeats the purpose of being a writer. Writers write because they want other people to know what they have discovered on their journeys.

What they discover might be beautiful beyond comprehension, or more terrible than anything in our worst nightmares.

That is what this book is about. It's about discovering things that I didn't know I had in me. Some of them are wonderful, electric, beautiful (to me anyway), and I hope the reader will agree; others are less savoury in nature, and I hope the reader will understand that too. I make no apology for writing what I write, because I could not write honestly about life or people if I did not include some of the unsavoury aspects of human life: rape, violence, sex, mutilation. All these things are present in this book, but there are things too that are good. I cannot lie and say these stories are not disturbing, they were disturbing to write. But I make no apology for them.

A created thing may have some basis in reality; but that does not mean that that reality need be based on the immediate reality of the creator: if that were the case, we would be asking any writers of detective fiction if they had been involved recently in any of the crimes we read about in their books!

In each of these strange stories, I have endeavoured to discover something, much like an archaeologist, and some of the things I have discovered have surprised me. It turns out I have a knack for twisting fairy tales into something almost unrecognizable, which isn't so bad. Any story with conventions can be made into something interesting, and worth looking at. I hope you enjoy this frightening (though long) story, as much as I enjoyed the writing and the rewriting of it.

My taste for folklore has not diminished either. I wrote a savage tale with dinosaurs in it. These animals have fascinated me since I was a child; indeed, they still capture my imagination like the day I first saw a painting of one: a dromaeosaurid with hooked claws on both feet, poised to pounce on a small lizard. I knew, somehow, that that lizard would not get out alive, and that claw would destroy the poor thing—I still hope the lizard took off like lightning before the fatal blow.

Victorian novels have been some of my favourite reading, even when I was young. They allow me to see not only the world in which these people lived and died, but how they thought and acted, and the secrets they concealed. The third story is a story about such secrets; about lies and the things that happen when we tell them, and how our actions affect the people we say we love. I wrote this story, in a strange mood, channelling, I think, the kind of energy Daphne du Maurier might have felt were she alive today. Undoubtedly, she would have looked at my story, give a sly, amused chuckle, and proceed to write the same story and do it infinitely better! I wrote this story for and dedicate it to Jamie McMurchie.

The last tale in this collection means a lot to me, as do all my stories—but this one remains the most personal. It was written as a surprise for Michael Walker—but I was devastated to learn of my friend's tragic death on the 23rd of September, and I never got the chance to share the story. After some rewriting, I have placed it where it belongs.

When we put pen to paper our friends find their way into our stories. Thus we make our friends immortal—in fiction they are always remembered, and though we cannot see them and cannot hear them, we can always feel them nearby.

My thanks to Michael Everson of Evertype, who so kindly gave me a chance to show the world some of my stories for the first time in printed form. I must thank, too, my beloved Edie Urquhart, who read many of these stories first, if not all of them; to Jasmine Masuod, who has been a constant help and encouraging factor whenever I have talked about my stories; to Callum McDonald, whose talks about mythology and literature and what can be done in it have been a source of endless entertainment and fascination; to Dan Kingston, who kindly gave me much needed advice when I showed him some stories to be put under the microscope, and who showed me the different angles from which I could tell each of the stories—there is nothing so wonderful as a director's eyes, when dealing with perspective in a story. And finally, to Robert Begg, who has been of immense help and encouragement, whose discussions on storytelling have been a constant inspiration and the most enlightening, and who has been so kind and patient whenever I felt I would give up.

Ryan Petrie
Dundee, Winter Solstice 2020

The Scarlet Petal

The Scarlet Petal

I

I shall never forget my father's face when he told me the losing hand was his. That bloodless, lipless mouth twitched when it spoke, like he expected me to strike him—and given the chance I might have done just that. But I am a lady; I know better than to strike my own father in anger. I would let his agony stretch in a way I deemed better than any blow I might have dealt: I wanted him to feel shame, a shame that was so very plain on his face when he entered my room, the same shame I hoped would drive him to use his service revolver on himself and make me an orphan.

A wicked child you can call me; a wicked child I became that night.

I sat in the carriage opposite *la Bête*, and tried to stare at anything but his face, a face hidden by the shiny film of a porcelain mask, rouged cheeks, sweet-scented hair for a wig, and slots in the mask where his eyes fixed on me with a piercing look. I did my best to avoid those eyes—it was all one could ever do. He did not speak and I did not invite conversation; I spent my time looking out the carriage window, watching the world and all its wonderous treasure go by, pastures where cows and sheep grazed happily, where farmers and their boys were going about their daily work as they had done for hundreds of years, never conscious of the monsters that lived nearby, or if they did they took no notice of them. I was jealous of their ignorance.

The transaction was a quick one. I was only given a night to prepare. Prepare to leave this cottage on the sea, prepare for my new life of servitude to a master I knew had no love for me, not like my captain's son who fought for me the night of the game of cards, the game in which my father lost me, his only daughter.

La Bête had promised my father an annuity, a sum which he could not have thought of in his wildest dreams, a sum that would erase his debts and settle him for life. And there would be no me to nag him as I had done before, when we had no money, no pride, no honour to speak of. Our family name was a source of gentle embarrassment to the other great families of France. No doubt they sat in their lounges and talked about us, in the way the rich do when one of their kind has fallen from grace, and they treated us as a sort of parable, a fable which their children would learn by heart so that they would never spoil their family wealth, or they would end up like us: poor, desperate, and laughed at from afar when the hand of charity was offered with a smiling face.

My father wondered how he could pay such a sum back, but *la Bête* said, "It is one of the wisest proverbs, I think, to never question the kindness of a friend. It is bad karma."

My father did not question it again. He took the money and was rid of me.

I let my mind drift. How we came to be in such a position is all too common in English novels: the father in grave financial debt, owes his creditors more than he can give, and spends a considerable amount of money than can be replaced. He would make no effort to retrench, such a life as his was bought and paid for, and he paid a good deal for it. I would not contradict him. His lifestyle was mine, and I shared, though to a lesser extent, his vices.

I was fond of nice things and I liked having them around me. Gowns and books were my greatest joys, and any new material or dress that was now the fashion in Paris had to be procured and showed off. My friends and I revelled in beads and silks and stockings. Our sin was of vanity. Though I loved to dress in expensive things, I knew this was the one sacrifice I had to make, if we were to make any positive change to our situation. In times like those, I thought often of my mother.

She was a brave, gentle soul who had a mind for mathematics. I like to think I inherited some of her spirit, and her common sense, but I can make no claim of the kind. If I could, we would not have been in such a situation—the same could be said if I had her strength to say "no" when my father went on one of his spectacular sprees in Paris.

There is no chance of me being anything like those virtuous heroines you read of in Jane Austen novels, for they had not the vices and avarices I had then and to some degree still possess.

When my mother was alive there was control; and with her absence our control diminished, and we destroyed ourselves. Our lesson was hard-learned, but I would not have it any other way. She would not let him toe any lines, would not let him be seen dead near a money lender's den. But he would find himself in their clutches, and ever would they be ready to close on their pound of flesh. And he would spend—oh yes, he would spend money like water, finding he would have less than he thought when he left the house in Paris and found himself in another den of sin and gambling, letting his sickness overcome him, overwhelm him till the last dregs of my inheritance were wrung from him. The cards were a cruel mistress, and she often had her men hold him down while his purse was unceremoniously raped of its wares. Notes and coins, all pinched from him until he was left with nothing.

The news of his great betrayal came as a shock to us all. Our servants could not be paid, the landowners would give nothing, and we had no power to punish them for their insolence, for though we were the family that owned their houses, we had no power to turn them away.

"What money would be in it if you do?" they said. "What money is there kicking us out?"

To this my father had no answer. He told them to go and sat in his chair with his face in his hands.

It was painful to watch him so fallen. Here sat a man who once stood tall and proud with long dark hair which he kept tied back with a velvet ribbon of midnight blue, and whose face lit up a room with a smile. This was the face that caught the eye of Madeleine de Longforte, daughter of the Marquis de Longforte, one of the richest families in France. Here it seemed there was a good match, and for a long time it was. Nothing could separate them, and the appearance of a child seemed to cement the union.

Our home was one of light and music and happiness, until my father's vices and habits were discovered. He laid his luck in cards and his love of drink was just as strong. Madeleine did not know what to do. Pleading with him was no use, and there was no need for scandal. They lived separate lives, and I between them both, loving my father's frivolities and never understanding, until too late, the damage they would ultimately inflict on us, and my mother's quiet, sensible manners. I wish now that something different occurred, or that Papa died instead of Maman.

We females can survive without the use of a man, and we have more of a head for sums and figures. We have spent years living carefully on so little, yet it is never to our credit. We live longer, it seems, than a man might when we have so little. Is it perhaps this inherent skill that we know what is best needed than men do?

It was now my turn to look after this man who sobbed like a child, unsure of what to do next, cursing the cruelty of the world when the world dealt him the only hand she had left— the hand she had no choice but to give. Our estate was threatened with foreclosure, and our only hope was to invite wealthy visitors to stay. We would rent the house and stay away for a little while. That scheme had worked before when other families were in the same difficulty so we would do the same.

A family was found and they would take up residence within the week.

The family lawyer was present at the signing of the lease and the document was thought satisfactory. We would remain a few more days and consider other places to stay, as we did not want to be in the way of the new family. Our house, though big enough for both, would never have suited my father's pride in having to share; not even in the days of the war would he have allowed anyone to share his ancestral home. Napoleon himself would be turned from the door.

We met the newcomers a few times during our last few days there. The Lerouxs were a beautiful family from a long line of sailors and admirals—the chief was an admiral himself and in full command, as any admiral would be. He was a benevolent soul and loved gardens, and loved best of all to walk with his wife by the rose bushes; his son, a handsome gentleman with high cheekbones and a tender disposition, said that it reminded them of their old courtship, that when they walked in a rose garden they were taken back to the day his father proposed to his mother and she accepted. I could not help but feel tears start in my eyes to the romanticism of it.

The admiral's son introduced himself as Adam Leroux, and I gave my name, which he commented was the loveliest he had ever heard. I blushed to his compliments as any young girl would when she is attracted.

After three days, it was announced that a house had been found. A cottage outside Calais where we would have only a few servants and a cook, who would go on ahead and make things ready for us: my father heartily agreed, saying that the sea would probably cure him of this illness that had taken over his as well as all our lives. Though I was very much in favour of the trip, it felt forlorn that I had to leave my new friend so soon. I told him the news when I saw him last and explained that it would be for the duration. There was no point in lying to him about our situation, so I told him outright. He listened without judgement, though there was a wince or two as I gave him the particulars. His only question was, "When will I see you again?"

I replied with misty eyes that I did not know, but hoped it would be soon.

It was that moment, in the rose garden, like his parents before him, that we shared our first kiss. I blushed as anyone might when they are surprised in such a way. Almost at once he was apologetic, calling himself a rogue and a fiend for having presumed he had permission to kiss me. I soothed him as best I could, telling him that it was one of the sweetest things anyone had ever done for me. We kissed again and my cheeks burned scarlet. Attraction yes, love—no, not yet. There is a difference, and most fairy tales don't get it right.

But this was a sinful feeling, this love of his appearance, and the thoughts of what lay beneath that shirt and vest. I brought my mind back before I let it go too far, and parted with him in the garden. I stole a glance over my shoulder as he stared after me, a wide grin on his face, his curly hair falling over one eye.

We took some time getting ready, though I did not much mind. It gave me more time with my new friend and, I suppose, my lover. We spent another week in each other's company before news came that the cottage was ready for us.

The house in Paris had been sold, which gave us more than enough to purchase the new one, a house more easily managed than the last, requiring minimal staff too. I packed my clothes and books, such were my treasures, and a small portrait of Maman, which I took with me whenever I travelled, so she would rest on my bedside table and watch over me while I slept. Her presence was always a comforting thought.

There was a knock on my door. Adam poked his head through the gap and smiled. "I do not wish to be presumptuous," he said, "but may you spare me a few moments of your time for company?"

I begged him be seated and remarked that I was only packing. A maid was present, so nothing untoward could happen between us. I was glad she was there; no telling what might happen if she was not. But we talked long into the night, and lots of smiling and laughter took place. Some sadness was admitted to that we had to leave each other so soon after only recently becoming acquainted. I confessed my own sadness, but remarked that it would not be forever.

"I hope not," he said, "for it would be an honour and privilege to know you better…"

There was silence for some seconds, and I thought we would be pulled together and kiss like we had in the rose garden, but my maid said that it was getting late and that I needed my sleep.

I assented to this and the maid ushered him out. After some seconds and smiling like a fool, I realized that I had made a terrible mistake: I had let a man in my room and let him see me handle my garments. Shameful conduct on my part. What would my father say? He must never discover the truth, of course, even if nothing untoward happened between us. I turned to my girl and said, "You must never speak of what has happened here, do you understand."

"*Mais oui, mademoiselle*," said the maid, and my mind was put at ease.

Morning came and we packed our things into the carriage. We were given a send-off by the Lerouxs and the rest of the household staff. A short speech was given by my father that they would serve the Lerouxs until we came back, that they were to treat them with all kindness and civility as though we were still in the house and give them absolute loyalty. "They are part of the family now," my father said, "or soon will be."

I felt my cheeks colour at his remarks and did not look at him when we sat down as the carriage pulled away from the house. When we were far enough away, I put my head out the carriage window and watched the great house recede from view and turning a corner was obscured by the line of a hedgerow. I drew back in when I could not see the house or my lover any more.

As we made our way more toward Calais, we stopped a few times at very good inns and paid the landlords handsomely, but when we came to Paris, we spent more than we could really afford on hotel rooms that were beyond our means. Their hospitality was not to be sneezed at or turned away, said my father, when he booked for us the most expensive rooms. It was also at this hotel that the family lawyer caught up with us and gave us news that shocked as well as dismayed us. Our home had been besieged by creditors looking for Papa. The Lerouxs were able to pay the debt, though they expected some payment in return for their kindness. Papa was beside himself with wrath, though there was nothing he could do. He determined to return and make sure whoever was responsible paid for their crime.

"There is more," said the lawyer cautiously.

"More?" Papa snapped. "More? How can there be more? Have they not already added enough salt to injury, now that my tenants know of my disgrace?"

The lawyer went on, plainly nervous. I reached out a comforting hand and took his, gently stroking it with my thumb.

"Fear not, *monsieur*," I said, "you are with friends."

My father grew impatient with the lawyer's reluctance to speak, so I tried my best to soothe him and get what he wanted to say out.

"They have done some damage to your family portraits, *monsieur*," he said finally. My father's jaw dropped. "They have slashed every portrait of yourself and your family. But—" here he paused and wondered if he ought to go on. "They did not touch the portrait of yourself and your wife. They left that well alone. I was there when they were tearing the place apart and the Lerouxs were watching. The ruffian who led them all said, 'We leave her. *Oui*, we leave her well enough alone. He ought to remember how beautiful she is, and that the man who has her hand and disgraces her thus ought to die like a faithful dog to let her home be driven to shame.' He said nothing else and they all left. We were left standing speechless, but it is safe to assume the whole county knows of your misfortune, *monsieur*."

There was a long time of silence when my father got from his chair and left us. I went on eating my duck *à l'orange* while my companion ordered another bottle of wine to soothe his nerves.

It was a little while later that the lawyer and I parted and I went up to my room for bed. We had adjoining rooms, connected by a door, should my father need me. I would sneak through the door and come to his assistance when the time came. So far there was no need of me, only loud sobbing which I heard through the wall, and a knock on the door from the *garçon* with an expensive bottle of champagne. I tipped the boy and brought it to my father's room. I knocked gently on the door, went in, and left the champagne on the table. I didn't want to see him as he was, sobbing and wailing like a child who has lost his mother. It was too pathetic for me to stand. I locked my door when I went back to my room and got ready for bed.

I fell asleep not long after but woke with a start when I heard a loud cry from the other room. I got up and threw my dressing gown round my shoulders and unlocked the door. When I burst in, I saw my father on his bed, engaged in the act of lovemaking with another woman. Dumbness struck me still and I stared. The room was full of the noises of passion, and my father grunted like a wild animal. He looked up and stopped, but the woman kept going. She, with her mouth open looked at me upside down and gasped as she ground against him. She was rouged and looked the picture of a stage Marie Antoinette before she was deposed and sent to the guillotine. Two large red weals adorned her pale, deathly-white cheeks, and her teeth, what was left of them, could be seen stark white against the red of her mouth. My legs felt weak and I stumbled back into my room and closed the door. I was grateful for the solid oak I leant against but it was not enough.

There was a sickly feeling rising in me, like vomit. I had to rush to the *toilette* before anything reached my throat. I barely made it in time. After that I slipped beneath my blankets and drifted into a troubled sleep, the sounds of passion still ringing in my ears.

I dared not look him in the eye the next day, for I knew I would never be able to see him in any other light than what I saw him do. It seems silly to react to a man having his way with a woman, especially a woman for whom he has paid, but something hit me like it has never hit me before. He was sharing a bed with another woman other than Maman, and it hurt to see it. He would not look at me—indeed, he would not talk—when he came down for breakfast. When we were done, I said that we ought to make haste if we wanted to make for

Calais in good time. He got up and went back to his room; I consoled myself with the thought that it was not done in his own marital bed back home.

When we were ready, I made to tip the man at the desk but my father seized my arm and dragged me away. "We don't have time," he said. "A creditor has been warned of our presence here, we must leave at once!"

He shoved me into the carriage and slammed the door once he got in himself. We were off at speed. I had only a second to glance the wrathful face of the receptionist before he was lost to me forever. The carriage jolted and bumped on its way through Paris and we were thrown from one end to the other, jostled around and made to bounce like a little boy's ball. When we were free from Paris my father ordered the driver to maintain the speed, for the sooner we got to Calais the better—the lesser distractions there would be.

I would not meet his eyes still, and I knew he knew what I thought of him. We did not speak the whole way to Calais.

We arrived in haste and we met our new home with greater ease than we had a right to feel. But this quaint little place was lovely: the lawyer was right, it was more easily managed than the great house, and with so small a crew of staff, it would be more than adequate to spend our days there till things got better with our finances. There were no major shops here, and there was very little to do. A beach lay nearby, and we could sit there and watch the steamers as they went to and fro across the Channel to England and back. I felt a sudden wave of emotion grip me—I knew, somehow, that everything was going to be all right.

People say that deep in their bones they know something will come their way and it will be all right. And this I am in great accordance with. Some power exists that allows someone to know with absolute certainty that everything that has gone before is now at an end, and everything to come will bring nothing but great joy and happiness to themselves and others around them. I had an inkling that this house would be the making of us.

The servants who went before us to make the cottage liveable were here: Piotr, Colette, Marie, Sasha, Achille, and Madame Bambois. They were the most revered of our staff, and we had every confidence in their skills as people who could handle our household and make it a home. Madame Bambois was a personal favourite of mine—housekeeper of the last house, she was chosen to run this new ship, though she had none too many nice words to say about it: "Not what I am used to at all...too small...too close..." One could tell she was not a woman who liked being in close quarters with the people she worked with, even if the conditions back home were just as cramped downstairs.

After a few days' settling in, I announced to Madame Bambois that we ought to hold a very small celebration, invite anyone we knew in town, and ask if anyone we might know was present.

She shook her head sadly. "None that I would remember, *mademoiselle*," she said. "But I have a feeling that there is someone in town who might come to your gathering, though I don't much like the sounds of him."

I was confused and somewhat taken aback, for Madame Bambois never expressed her dislike for anyone, even those on her own staff. She deigned to work with them civilly, but to hear her talking about someone who was not staff was quite a shock.

"Not that I mean to gossip," she went on hurriedly. "Only, since we arrived, we've heard tell of this person, a gentleman—if he can be called that—who lurks the scene here. He's not too good a gentleman, cantankerous to boot and drives people to distraction when he's in a room, so I have heard."

"Does he have a name?" I asked.

"I've only ever heard him called *la Bête, mademoiselle*," she replied.

La Bête

The Beast.

I let Madame Bambois get on with her work and considered a few moments as I sat in the small library room, where I decided to place my office, if I were to help with maintaining the house and our income like my mother before me—the name worked on me and I did not know why.

I thought, *We shall see what he is like when he comes.*

And he did come, the night of the party, where some eight of our guests had already arrived on time, and we were sitting down to cards. My father, always an eager host, watched them as they played, though he did not take up a deck. The sickness was still strong in him, and any relapse might prove our doom. The door gave a great thud, as though someone had taken a hammer to a panel. Our guests started and the ladies began to quiver.

The next moment our new arrival stood in the doorway after having some difficulty squeezing through. He was impossibly tall and almost as impossibly wide, though not with fat: his Juggernaut form was composed entirely of muscle: his clothes were the finest silks and cloths to be found in Paris, and his wig was fragranced with a perfume I did not recognize. The last feature I want to record, though it was the first that drew our attention, is his mask. Porcelain, sleek, lightly rouged at the cheeks, with eyeholes through which burned two bright blue eyes.

"*Mesdames et messieurs,*" said Piotr, dwarfed by this monstrous being who stood in our parlour, "*la Bête...*"

II

I wish I could record all I remember of that night, but I cannot. It is impossible, more for the reasons that I have deliberately tried to forget. In some ways it has worked, in others I am not so fortunate. I recall the feeling of being watched the whole night, the unease that filled the room when he set himself on a sofa, and it creaked under his weight. The woman next to him shifted uncomfortably but did not have the courage to move away from him.

When it was all over and I lay in bed, I cast my mind back to those eyes: icy-blue, the kind of eyes that delve deep into one's heart and tries to find the secrets it holds. They were scrutinous eyes, invasive eyes, eyes you never want to have looking at you because you know they are undressing you mentally. When his gaze cast over me, I felt that peculiar tension, that sense of invasion I had never felt before. There is admiring and there is plain ogling, and his gaze fell to the latter. After that, my mind went back to his mask, that terrible mask that feigned humanity with its colouring, but it was humanity barely attained, it glistened and any illusion that it might be human was shattered. His breathing was laboured—perhaps being in a room full of women and their men brought some pleasure to him, their unease brought him merriment too, for when he sat next to the woman and he put his arm around her, her husband made to protest and got to his feet. *La Bête* merely looked at him, and the lady's husband resumed his seat. Our newcomer laughed, and got to talking with his companion.

Morning came and all was cleared away. Our guests who had opted to stay the night had now left and we were given gracious thanks. Breakfast after a party is always a cheerful occasion: when one knows that their get-together has been a success and everyone has enjoyed themselves—the only hitch, one could say, was *la Bête*. Whoever he was, we were sure to never invite him to another party. Our guests' welfare was important to us, and if he was able to take a snub, then he would take it with no complaint. Indeed, I thought that the snub would give him immense satisfaction, that his presence made the new neighbours more than uncomfortable and his presence at our table was not appreciated. Some people delight in the misery of others and in causing trouble of this kind; it's a wonder they don't destroy themselves doing so.

Letters were received and opened. Friends of the family wished us all the best in our new home, that our situation would soon smooth over and we would return in no time.

I received word from my friends; they were eager to see me and I missed them very much. We used to spend a lot of time together, and in memory of those occasions, they would make gifts of the latest Paris fabrics and bring them to me for inspection. I would not have to pay a penny: "Think of it," they said, "as a homecoming present." I wrote back with haste that whenever they were in the area, they should drop in. They did, after a time. And we spent much time drinking tea and examining the gown brought me for inspection. How sumptuous they looked, how divine: the silk ran through my hands like water, my fingers sensitive to the touch. We laughed a good deal too, then the topic of conversation turned to that of boys.

You can imagine my face when boys were mentioned, and my friends talked incessantly about the most eligible men in Paris—students with wealthy families, aristocrats seen in the family pews in church, or seen in the audiences of the opera house. They giggled and swooned over their fairy tale princes—one of them had an eye on a gentleman who reciprocated her desire. Very soon, she said, an engagement might come of it, though she was unsure of how her father would react, or how his family would see the romance between them. My friend was of a lower station, though she was of good family and with many connections; but that does not count for much when one has so many tens of thousands of livres a year and several estates in the country and a house in the City.

"What about you?" they said turning to me. "Is there anyone who has caught your eye?"

My cheeks coloured and grew hot. They egged me on and begged me to tell them who; I gave them the particulars and told them that we had kissed. This drew gasps from a few of them but they were all wide-eyed. None of them had ever got that far and they were jealous.

"Does your father know?"

The thought horrified me. "Certainly not," I said. "We only kissed, though I think there was an attachment forming. We nearly kissed a second time, but he was ejected from my room." Now the girls were scandalized. I hastened to add, "Nothing happened. We were just talking. I had a maid with me, helping me pack to come here. We talked and laughed, but I thought at the end of it that we would…then the maid said that I needed to get sleep. I think that if she wasn't there, we might have."

"So very sweet," they chorused. I couldn't help but feel a little invaded, that my privacy had been violated, but I let it pass. They were my friends. We shared everything, even our most delicious secrets.

Several more days passed and I received a letter from Adam. My knees nearly buckled and I hurried to my room to read it properly. My father was concerned and came to my room. I assured him that I was quite well, but that I had received news from the son of Admiral Leroux. Papa was delighted and said that he must be invited to spend time with us, now that we were in a more stable situation, and our finances, from what our lawyer wrote, were greatly improved. I wrote in haste and sent it by the last post, hoping he would receive it in time.

Time went by and we had more parties, and we were glad that *la Bête* appreciated that he was not wanted there. He did not turn up unannounced, did not intrude on us, did not even send us a letter of complaint. I could not get out of my head the thought that he was rocking in his chair with laughter, relishing in the fact that he was hated and feared. Why some men enjoy being feared and hated, I don't know. It is a peculiar indulgence that will never be explained.

After a week, Adam Leroux arrived at our house and I greeted him warmly. At dinner we talked a good deal, during the day he took me around Calais. We went to the beach, Adam, myself, and Papa. Papa had not been to the beach in so long, had not even a bathing suit. But we did not mind. Papa sat in his sun chair and basked. Adam and I went walking along the stretch of sand, our feet bare and letting the water rush over them. It was cold against my skin.

In the distance a steamer passed by, black smoke billowing from its funnel.

We talked of our childhoods, and he told me that he wanted to be an artist. Admiral Leroux did not approve, but his mother encouraged it—yes, that good woman was more than what they deserved as a family, as most mothers are. "Fathers," he said, "seem to be a great deal more trouble than they are worth."

I made no reply to this, and I think he caught on. He made hasty apologies, saying that he did not mean it in an unkind fashion. I laughed and soothed him. "There is no need to apologize for what is true," I said. "But he is getting better. That at least can be granted him." We said no more on the subject and went on walking along the beach.

Our return was later than we expected, and we were greeted with an unpleasant surprise. *La Bête* was waiting for us. He sat in the lounge and stood when we entered the room. My father took his hand, which was the size of a large ham, and my father's hand disappeared in its folds. He spoke with my father in a confident, sporting manner, then turned to me and offered his hand. I let him take it with some reluctance. He pressed my hand to his porcelain lips—they were cold, like a corpse. I resisted the urge to retract and hide behind my friend.

When he spotted Adam Leroux, he straightened and his manner became hard and cold.

"And who is this strapping, fine fellow?" he asked impertinently.

My father made introductions, and Adam extended his hand, but *la Bête* would not take it.

"Would I be so presumptuous as to ask for a few moments of your time, sir?" he said to my father. He nodded. Adam and I left the room.

An hour or two passed, and we waited with great anxiety. What did he want? Adam took my hands in his and did his best to soothe me. The door of the lounge opened, and *la Bête* came out. He regarded us passively and gave a snorting chuckle before he headed for the door.

I hurried into the room and my father sat on the sofa, his face drained of colour and his body shaking.

"Our guest has demanded a game," he said. "A game of cards."

I could not believe what I was hearing—he had been doing so well. Why did he have to jeopardize our futures now?

"What are the stakes?" I demanded.

"No money, no rights to land, no properties," Papa said. "If he wins, he wants you."

The words crashed down on me, the world went still and there was silence for what felt like forever. My father had bet me as the stakes at a game of cards...

I would not speak to him that whole night, would not deign to share the same room, but Adam was always with me, always holding my hand, holding me to his chest when I burst into fits of hysterical tears. His was the presence I cherished most during that uncertainty. I don't know what I would have done without him. Perhaps I would be dead, would have run away and headed for the beach, ready to drown myself; or would I have thrown myself from a window and hoped I landed on the patio head-first so that my neck would snap.

La Bête returned later that evening—some guests were brought, friends of his who would cheer on either side. Bets were made as to the winner. I dressed for a party; I wanted to be present so that my father was reminded of what was at stake, so that frivolity would not overcome him, and he would not take any risks that would cost him his daughter.

I will not speak of the game, for it would take too long to discuss how he lost, but lose he did and I was told to be ready in the morning. I would be taken off my father's hands while he was handsomely compensated. He was to move to England, and never set foot on the shores of France again. A steep price to pay for one who was now suddenly so rich. I was sent to my room and forced to pack.

Below me was the sounds of a fierce argument—Adam's voice sounded, and I heard words pass between them I did not think possible for either to say. My lover's voice was consistently raised, angry, indignant that any father would have been so foolish as to stake his daughter against a fiend; my father's voice was low, subdued. I snuck down the stairs to listen to what they were saying, Adam's voice was so loud that I could not make out much of his speech, but my father's reply was cool and clear: "I will not renege on an agreement once made. It is not gentlemanly."

"Not gentlemanly," said Adam softly, I could hear his breath coming hard, his nostrils flaring, his body shaking as he stared at my father. "*This* is ungentlemanly. Your daughter had a price, and you lost it. But now you are so handsomely rewarded for your loss, you do not care."

My father stood to protest; his mouth opened but no words came. Then he saw me standing in the crack of the door. Adam turned to face me. Our eyes met for a second but I turned mine away. There was nothing to be done. My father would not break his word to our winner. Then I heard Adam say, "What man is so careless with his treasures that he gives them away thus? You should be ashamed of yourself. And her mother would be just as horrified."

That struck a nerve and I heard my father's rising anger, a raging voice and the sound of a vase exploding against a wall. "Get out! Get out of this house!"

My lover made no hesitation in leaving, but before he went out the door he turned and looked up at me as I stood on the stairs: "I will find a way to stop this. I promise you, *ma chère*."

With that he was gone.

Packing took longer than I thought it would. I was constantly interrupted by a continual flow of tears, and they stained some of my best gowns. I picked up the portrait of Maman and stared at her for a long time, the tears dripping from my chin onto the glass. I prayed for someone to come, for her to come and put her arms around me and tell me it was all going to be all right—but I did not get that wish. The dead rarely come to those who are living, and when we recall them in times of great trouble, there is nothing more they can do than provide for us little nuggets of knowledge from the past. We would ask them, "How would you have handled this?"

But I think we would often be disappointed with the answers. We don't know how they would have handled it— they had never witnessed it. Had they only heard of it in fairy tales? Did fathers sell their daughters at games of cards willy-nilly in their day? Or was it still this dark sickness which desperately needed to be cured?

There was a knock on the door and my father came in. He stood over me trying to be benevolent. If he spoke, I am sure I would have killed him; if he tried to say that I would have a better life with *la Bête* than I would have with him, I would have taken the pen from the desk and stuck it in his throat. But I did none of those things, because I am a lady. And my father did speak, and I hated him for it. He did say there would be a better life for me with my winner than with my own father. I snapped at last when I replied, "But you did not know you were stealing happiness from me when you bet me."

His face confessed his confusion. I told him that I had fallen in love with Adam Leroux, that I wanted to be his wife, that he felt the same for me as I did for him. But now I was bought and paid for, I was to be miserable and unloved, by a creature, not a gentleman, who would ogle me for the rest of his days. "You have sold me," I went on, "not as a bride, but as a trophy to the thing you lost me to. It is not enough that the great families of France talk about us as a parable to self-control, but they will now know us as the people who would sell our daughters and sons for any measure of gold. That is the legacy you leave me. That is what you will be remembered for."

He said nothing, but turned and left the room.

When dawn came, I rose and asked that a bath be run for me. I would breakfast early and dress in my finest garments of mourning. My maid asked why I would wear my funereal garb, and I said that I am an orphan. Any child who is sold is bereft of parentage, for that parent does not want their child.

The maid nodded and bobbed a curtsey. I wondered, too, if I heard her give a soft, pitiful sob when she left. If she did, then she was the only one to cry the entire time I was awake.

Papa did not join me for breakfast; I was glad, for the state of my dress would have caused considerable argument, and comments that I was still his daughter, and I would look on the brighter side of this transaction, for transaction it was.

I was experiencing a change of hands, a change of ownership, and I was to be treated and done with as my new master saw fit.

I stood on the steps for the carriage to take me away; as I waited, I gave one look to the place I loved. A curtain trembled for an instant. I was being watched. If it was my father, I resolved to not look again. When I stepped into that carriage, it would be the last thing he ever saw, that I would not show my face to him—the face he would soon forget now he was among his riches. You may think I judge my father too harshly, but fathers do not sell their children.

From a corner the carriage came, a gigantic thing with black casement and gold rims. I had never seen so ornate a vehicle, not even when royalty passed us by in Paris. The door opened when the carriage came to a stop; my host was inside, his gargantuan form filling in the space at one end of the carriage, his head ducked uncomfortably so that his head thrust forward slightly.

"Come, my dear," he said. "There is a long journey ahead of us."

I hesitated on the brink, resisting the urge to turn and bang on the door for my father. My resolve was strong. I would not be seen to be weak, not in front of my new owner. I took to the step and set myself into the carriage. My luggage was lashed to the roof and we were off at speed. We rode in silence for most of the trip.

Through cities and towns, villages and hamlets, stopping every now and then whenever my companion or myself needed our *toilette*, we carried on very much the whole day. My rear was getting numb sitting there as long as we did, and I found it incredibly uncomfortable that my host kept staring at me. Irritation rose within me and I was compelled to say, "If you wish to say something, *monsieur*, kindly say it. I do not like to be gawked at, like you have never seen a woman before."

This brought a barking laugh from my host.

"You have spirit," he said. "I like that in a girl. Spirit means a challenge, and challenges are what I enjoy most of all."

"Then I propose to be very challenging for you, *monsieur*; if not in strength, then in my wit."

He chuckled again and sat back in his chair.

We passed over bare country and finally came to the forests that rim the mountains at the heart of our beautiful land, where pines and spruce tower over all and stand rigid as soldiers at attention. Sunlight streamed through breaks in the canopy above, and birds called to one another, watching as the great carriage passed through their kingdom.

My companion said, "Not long now. We are almost home."

I looked out the window and admired the great trees, all straight and proud, not a single one diminished or struggling with its brother fighting for light, twisting itself for want of this precious commodity—all of them, beautiful and strange. My view was promptly obscured by the sudden entrance of the carriage into a tunnel. I started back and the Beast laughed. "Not to worry, my pet. Not to worry." But his words did little to soothe my fears. Where were we going? Where did this tunnel lead?

After a short while we were greeted once again by sunlight, and a new view was given us. We were travelling the edge of a deep gorge, and all around were waterfalls that trickled and fed a vein-thin river at the bottom with frothing rapids crashing against rocks. My captor heaved a great sigh and seemed to relax. He peered out of the window and if he could, I think he smiled behind the mask.

"There," he said, "there is home." He pointed to the far end of the gorge where a great castle carved of the rock stood, with waterfalls about it. My jaw hung open in astonishment.

I had never heard tell of such a place before—or perhaps I had, but only in fairy tales. I certainly could never remember there being any record of such a castle in the history of France, if it were, then it would have been written of extensively. Yet here it stood, in obscurity amid its mountains, surrounded by waterfalls, and a long winding road that curved round the cliff-face, and protected by a sheer drop down to the rushing river below.

Following the cliff path, we found ourselves coming to the great bridge that led to the castle's portcullis. I dare not look down when we crossed, for I knew I would panic and would not leave the carriage. I closed my eyes and prayed for it to be over. My host chuckled when the carriage came to a halt with a slight bump. "We have arrived, *ma chère*. There is no need to be alarmed." I opened my eyes and found that we had stopped in a courtyard. The door opened and the Beast was the first to get out. He shoved me aside gently and squeezed through the tiny doorway with a grunt. He stumbled when he stepped onto the cobbled stones and cursed under his breath. Someone came forward and asked if he was all right and he snapped "Yes, of course I am. Get me inside, for God's sake."

He did not make an offer of his hand to help me from the carriage, not like any other gentleman. I stepped down and saw that a hand was held out for me. The driver had got down from untying my luggage from the roof and brought it down. "*Mademoiselle*," he said, "may I offer my assistance?"

I took it gratefully and stepped down. The courtyard was wide and full of figures, and there were many voices, mostly female. They gathered round him with bonneted heads and long magenta dresses, the garb of servitude. The horses, sleek black things with coats as shiny as ink, were led away from the front door and the carriage was pulled with them. They held their heads high when they walked. Majestic beasts they were, and they knew it.

A girl came toward me and picked up my case and said, "I will take this to your room, *mademoiselle*."

I thanked her but did not know what else to say.

The Beast called back to me. "These girls will take you to your rooms. I trust you will want to join me for dinner, or has your journey tired you too much?"

"I will take some food in my room, thank you," I said. "I am very tired."

He turned to his ladies and barked orders at them. "Set to it," he said when he was done. He turned and swept up the stairs with a cloak trailing behind him. "I will be in my rooms," he announced. "I do not wish for anyone to disturb me, is that clear?"

There was silent assent among the maids and he was gone.

I stood there dumbfounded, looking up at the immensity of the place.

The lobby, once we got inside, was resplendent beyond anything I had ever seen before. I had, in my youth, seen the beauty of Versailles, but from a distance. This defied even that in its grandeur. On the far wall above the great marble stairs, a massive stained-glass window shone with the light of the sun, spreading a kaleidoscope of colours onto the floor. I remembered, too, the Rose Window of Notre-Dame, and had to keep from crossing myself. Such a motion at this time would be silly. My Catholic faith had not been present or acknowledged since Maman passed on. This window inspired in me the urge to recognize it again, make an effort to connect to the merciful *bon Dieu* who delivers us all from evil. I prayed now He would deliver me from this fiend.

Up the stairs and to the left, I was showed to my rooms.

They were the size of a large apartment in Paris, with adjoining rooms: three in all. The first was the lounge, which made the bulk of the space, with divans and sofas, bookcases and a pianoforte, a large marble fireplace and many portraits. There were three tall, narrow windows that looked out over the falls. The other two rooms were the bedroom and the bathroom; the former had a large four-poster bed, the kind all too common in the last century, another sofa and a fireplace. This one had been lit.

My bathroom had all the majesty of a palace. Like the stairs it was carved entirely of marble, and the tub was ready for me, full and steaming. "We thought it best if we ran you one," said one of the maids. "It must have been a long journey for you, *mademoiselle*, and we thought you would wish for one before you went down to dinner."

"I am not going down to dinner," I said. "But I will gladly take the bath, thank you."

"Then we shall not trouble you, *mademoiselle*," they said, though they appointed me a lady in waiting, a bright red-headed girl called Amélie. She slipped my clothes from me with nimble dexterity. I wondered how long she had been here in service, for I noticed her hands. They were not the calloused, rough hands of a servant, but the smooth, clean hands of a girl who has never seen a day's work. They were delicate, small hands, hands used to cross-stitch, to play the piano. While I bathed, I asked my companion whether I ought to know anything about the castle or about my host that would be useful. If there were any rules I ought to observe, I would determine to be civil and follow them with minimum inconvenience, even if it meant I never left my room.

"There is nothing I can say, *mademoiselle*," she said, "nothing than what the master has already told you. Do not disturb him when he is in his chambers."

I nodded and lay in the tub in silence. Then the girl began to cry, her face in her hands and her shoulders heaving with the sobs.

"You should not be here," she said at last. "He promised there would be no more."

"No more what?" I said, sitting up and reaching out a comforting hand.

"He promised he would not bring any more women to this place. It is cruel, shameful! He has broken his promise. Now we must suffer another…"

I sat up and said firmly that I did not choose this. I gave her the story that my father had sold me to the Beast by losing me to cards. Amélie stared at me with wide eyes. "Worse it is, that a father should lose his daughter to him. He collects us, you see. And when he is bored with us, he summons us to his chambers."

She seemed to wait for me to question her, but I did not. She went on anyway. "He summons us and does things."

"You mean, he rapes you?"

She shook her head. "No, he has never touched me. But the things I have heard…"

Again, she faltered. I did my best to get it out of her, but she would not stop crying. After a while, she mastered herself and said: "When we are called to clean his chambers, there are always clothes, stained clothes, and lots of blood…Those who wore them are vanished. We do not know where they go. But we find trinkets of theirs, pieces left behind. He does not kill them; no, he is too vicious for that. He destroys them, *mademoiselle*, and, I think, he consumes them."

I felt the urge to vomit rise in my throat. My body shivered, even in the heat of the bath water.

When I was dried and my dressing gown was wrapped round me, food came through the door and was placed on my dressing table. I thanked the girls who brought it, who curtsied and were gone in an instant.

As I ate, I heard strange fumbling noises from outside. I did not rise immediately to investigate, but thought that a maid was working by my door. I thought I would leave her to her work. The fumbling went on, and a growl could be heard. A grunt of satisfaction and silence. My blood ran cold. Whoever it was had gone. I waited a short while and opened my door, and saw that a wet, glistening fluid trickled down the panels. I put my hand over my mouth and slammed the door shut.

I was in the home of a perverted madman—my life was in danger. He was a deviant, a monster who delighted in the pain and mutilation of women. I slammed the bolt-lock home and stepped back from the door.

When I was in bed, I heard again the fumbling and grunts of passion. I wrapped my pillow round my head to blot out the sounds he made, for I knew it was him. What other man was there in this castle that would have such manners, such gall as to do this outside a woman's door?

Amélie's words rang in my ears the whole night: *he destroys them, mademoiselle, and, I think, he consumes them...*

My dreams were haunted by visions of rape, of his rigid member forcing itself into me, and of sharp, human teeth sinking into my flesh, tearing it away from the bone. I cried out in the night but found my room empty and dark.

I lit a lamp and hurried into the other room, looking for a book. Jane Austen is always a good choice when in a crisis; one wonders: what would her heroines do? So, I took a copy of her best work and returned to bed, and lost myself in the worlds of books, pretending to be the heroine of a grand adventure. My handsome prince would come riding in on his steed to win the day. I would take his hand and we would ride off on horseback into the sunset—there would be no need to fight the Beast, he would be honourable and know when he is defeated—and in the end, we would be married. And the face of my prince was always Adam's face. I looked up at his handsome, smiling features while we rode away to happiness. It was too much for me then. I closed the book, settled down, and started to cry for what I had lost.

III

I could not stay in my room indefinitely. One day or another I would have to come out and face him, though the idea repulsed me. But face him I did. I came out of the room and found him waiting for me on the other side of the door, watching me. I could sense great glee in his being, and his eyes burned bright blue; I could see two pricks of light in the holes of his mask.

This mask was different, for it had a large hole where the mouth ought to be. He smoked a cigar through it and let it hang between his lips.

"How good of you," he said at last, "to grace us with your presence."

I made to reply but thought better of it. Why should I rise to his game?

He laughed.

"Fret not, I shall not harm you."

"Indeed, though you would pester me in the night, no less."

This caught him off-guard.

"I am afraid I don't understand you."

I bade him come, severe, almost like a mother who has caught her child doing something very naughty. He approached. I pointed to the stained panels of my door. "You are not responsible for this? I know of no other man in this castle who has the ability to do such, unless your driver has found a way to sneak into the castle when it is dark to come to my room and pay me these compliments? I say to you, sir, that you are base in these actions."

He surveyed the door and his eyes blazed with fury. But he did not look at me; it was as if he looked beyond me and went storming down the passage. There was not another word said between us. Amélie came from the other end of the corridor and gave me a fright. She said she was sorry, and told me that a lunch was laid out for me. "Would you like me to bring some up?"

"No, I shall lunch downstairs, today," I said. "I cannot hide in that room forever, waiting for what must come."

I did not expect her to say "You are so brave, *mademoiselle*," there was no need. I was not brave, nor did I want to be considered thus. I only wanted out of this great carved dungeon stuffed with relics that history had passed by and never thought to mention. So much here that I had only thought existed in stories and conspiracy—here they were, unknown paintings by the most famous of their day. A complete da Vinci, the story of Leida and Jove in the form of a swam before he raped her—the irony was too much for me and I avoided it wherever possible. Suits of armour lined the corridor and their heads turned when I passed by. I think they thought I did not notice, for they turned right away again when I looked on them.

This was place taunted newcomers, and the magic here started to work its mischief, mocking me. I did not mind much, the pain of my situation having lost its sting; I felt that no other mockery could possibly hurt me. But the pearly leavings on my door, the essence of perverted minds, that was an insult I would not let rest and one which would not be borne. Someone would pay for it, and my words to the Beast, clipped, pointed, made sure I would not tolerate such from any man, no matter if he owned me. But his reaction was strange, unexpected. I did not think he would deny it, nor did I think he would storm off as he did. I thought, rather, he would gloat over such obscene behaviour, but he did not.

The anger in his eyes was genuine enough. I had seen it often on the faces of those who have had insults thrown and falsehoods spread when they are baseless. But insult and falsehood need no base for survival: they thrive even when there is no food for them, they grow fat on uncertainty.

At once I was certain, but now there was doubt. What if it wasn't him who had paid me those nightly visits and desecrated my door? What if it was indeed someone else? Shame welled in me, accusing him of something he had not done; my mind snapped back to reality, ridding itself of such delusions. My host was a monster who consumed his staff when his temper was high. He would kill me as certainly as he would have killed anyone else, as certainly as he murdered the other women of his house.

I reached the stairs and descended them. The great lobby was empty save for two girls at their work. They chatted for a bit; when they saw me, they fell silent. I suppose they thought that if I had caught them whispering, I might report them. I said nothing, of course. But in my head, I promised them silence. I would not betray my sisters to this fiend, and I hoped they somehow heard the thoughts in my head. I thought also of their jealousy, their snide, malicious thoughts towards this outsider, newly arrived after a promise broken. Their resentment would be shown me, I was sure. And I could not blame them for it.

These were strange circumstances to be under. In anything resembling normality, they would have been dismissed and sent away. But they could not be sent away; they were not here of their own volition like most household staff.

The door to the dining room was open. Inside, a fire had been lit.

When I got to the door, I saw the table set and a variety of food laid out for me. Salads and cold meats, salvers of biscuits and sandwiches, and cooked things, too, had been provided. It was strange, seeing the table laid before me as it was, after having spent so long being so careful with money, and rationing ourselves, our table not what we were used to. I had grown so accustomed to the forced scarcity, the inability to indulge in my gluttonous habits. My stomach rumbled when I saw the plates ready for me. I took my seat and started heaping my plate high with my favourite things.

The food was quite delectable; everything made and cooked to perfection. The Beast knew how to keep a good table. Then I thought, *This table has enough food to keep a starving village for a week. What does he do with the things left behind?* But such thoughts left my head once again as I sank my teeth into the wing of a cooked fowl.

"I see you enjoy the food from my table," said a familiar voice from behind me.

My stomach churned over and turned icy and heavy. I felt suddenly sick. I wiped my lips and got to my feet but the Beast said, "Please, don't get up on my account. Continue with your feast. You must be famished after having spent so much time alone in that room. I knew you would want company at some point. It is a lonely place, I grant you. But it suits my purposes adequately."

I did not respond but went on eating, as he bade me.

We were silent for a few moments, then he sat in his chair and leaned back. He had a new cigar balancing in the hole of his mask.

"How do you like your rooms?" he said. "Are they comfortable enough?"

More than comfortable, I replied. I told him that they were beautifully furnished; I loved the bathroom most of all. He chuckled.

"Yes, the bathrooms seem to attract most of my guests, when they come." His voice was different, trailing off as if he knew that I knew he lied. He had no visitors, only the women he kept and the man he had as coachman. Another silence passed and finally he said, "I have discovered the 'pervert', as you call him, who has been paying you nightly visits. He has been dealt with and wishes to make a formal apology to you."

He snapped his fingers and there was the sound of shuffling feet behind me. A skulking creature with dark circles round his eyes stared at me from the side of the Beast's chair. He was young, no more than twenty-five, I thought, but his hair was streaked with grease and hung at strange angles, curling over his face. A gothic sight, I thought, a creature that was more likely to be found between headstones than as servant to a nobleman, no matter how ugly that nobleman may be in temper or taste. His podgy, pock-marked faced gave no impression that he was sorry, but his master had made a command, and he would fulfil it.

"My humblest apologies," he said, in a high, whining voice. "I assure you it won't happen again."

His presence disgusted me; the words I wanted to say stuck in my throat at the sight of him, but I managed to say: "I should hope not," and that was all.

Another snap of the master's fingers and he was off, skulking to whatever dark corner of the castle belonged to him.

"Once again," the Beast said, "I offer my sincerest apologies. Had I known that this was happening sooner, I might have spared you such unpleasant experiences. You must have lain uneasy in your bed this past week."

I conceded that I had. Then I did a strange thing, a silly thing. I gave my own apologies to the Beast, for accusing him of the acts. His regarded me in silence and if he could, I think he smiled. "You should not apologize for what your instinct and brain tell you. You hate me, and I understand why. I am a villain to you, and that is a role I am happy to live with for the time being. But never apologize for what your heart is screaming at you. It might, one day, save you."

We spoke no more than day.

Weeks passed, and I talked and dined with the Beast every day. We talked on every sort of subject that could be thought of. We argued and debated doctrine and God and the place of women. I rather think I won that debate, since it was one that he was eager to hear. I said, "What woman wishes to spend the rest of her days wed to a man who does not think of her as a woman, and only as a trophy; a receptacle for which he much give life so that a baby must be born? A woman wishes to make her own way in the world, to enjoy the freedoms men have so often denied them. How can you say our place is this or that, when it is also the place of men to hold to their promise made in marriage, that they will be true to their wives and ensure their protection? How many men do you know hold to that promise? How many women do you know crave freedom?"

This stung him, I think, for he sat back in his chair and regarded me.

For a second or two I thought he might relent. A fantasy went through my head that he would at last release us. Why, I don't know; a fantasy is a fantasy, in any regard. But he did not let us go. He kept us here, as I knew he would. I hoped against hope, but I thought perhaps he had found a new respect for myself and my sex.

The knowledge of his deeds notwithstanding, I thought that the best way to get into the Beast's head, and to change his ways was to get close to him. To present him with a challenge, as he put it, one he would gladly take up, one which would test his brain more than his brawn, a challenge he would find infinitely more difficult. I purposed to be like river water eroding an ancient stone. His member would not be the winner of these fights, and testing his intelligence proved more efficacious than I had originally anticipated.

He was skilled, oh yes; skilled in every way—but not so that he could be considered a prodigy. He was a voracious reader, and understood much of the sciences. His library, which he wanted to show me, consisted of a variety of volumes on dark arts, some he had searched through to find a cure for his condition. Yes, he told me that story, too. His transformation from man to Beast, the story of his mother, whom he adored.

"A brave, tender woman she was. Very kind, very peaceful. One of my many childhood treasures." His words struck me wrong, like he considered her property, like his father. Already, I thought, he had considered her the first woman he owned. "I was under her spell from the first," he said. "I would have done anything for her, and wanted to. I wanted to please her, to make her smile. I wanted her to shine radiance on me for ever, and make the world a bright and beautiful place. And she did, she did, *mon Dieu*. We went out to see the poor and needy, and when we were there, I would give the children my pennies, and give them the food from my pocket, knowing that they needed it more than I, but also with the calculation that she would see and she would scoop me in her arms and cherish me. I wanted desperately for her to be proud of me. You know how silly parents become when they see their children commit acts of kindness."

I remembered, indeed, going to see the poor with my own mother, how she cried for hours at my own acts of kindness towards those less fortunate than I. For the Beast and I had done the same thing: given our food and pennies to the poor children who needed it, and our mothers had received the action with the same loving tenderness and silliness over us. I smiled at the memory, and tears misted my eyes.

"Papa," he went on, "was a different kind of parent. So unlike Maman that it is impossible for me to think that they were ever in love. But she told me that they had loved."

There was a queer tremble in his voice as he spoke. These memories were painful.

"She believed that he still loved her, like she loved him. But it was impossible to love. A stalwart, ill-tempered man who liked his drink and his women. He often loudly asked, during their arguments, why he ever bothered to marry 'that Belgian whore', as he called Maman, on more than one occasion. He realized, as I did, that he had married her for her money. Then Maman fell ill. She never recovered. And during that illness, Papa would go to her room. The sounds I would hear were not human. It was impossible to believe that Maman had it in her to cry out like that, or that Papa could sound like a wild beast. When he gave those sharp cries, I knew it was over, and he would leave her alone. I went to her room once and tried to snuggle into her, to comfort her. But she pushed me away. She did not want me to see her thus. I left her, weeping. That night she went to sleep, and she never woke in the morning."

My lip trembled. I wanted to reach out a hand and touch his, but I stopped. My action did not go unnoticed, though he said nothing.

More weeks passed, and I had grown accustomed to our talks, his presence. But I did not grow accustomed to the creature that dangled on his coat-tails. La Marche was his name, and he had been in the service of the Beast since he was a boy; he didn't know who his father was. I don't think even the Beast knew, though I suspected he did not have a habit of remembering the people he killed. His mother was one of the maids here, though she too never made an appearance. My comfort in his presence lessened, and the Beast knew I was ill at ease with him there. When he sensed it, he sent him away, though La Marche was loath to leave his master's side.

One day he was insolent enough to refuse, and a great row burst out. The Beast gave a great bellowing roar, but La Marche did not flinch. He held fast and merely stared at his master before turning away and walking up the stairs.

I did not say anything when the Beast came to sit at the table for dinner.

We sat in silence, then I said, "Thank you."

He dismissed my thanks with a grunt and a wave of his hand, which then went over his mask as though he massaged the bridge of its nose.

"He should be gone," he said. "He should have died at birth, the wretch."

I was astounded by the unkindness of his words, but I did not blame him for them. I too indulged in the thoughts that his mother might have been a happier woman if the child had died at birth, something no woman wishes on another—we know the pain of that loss too well.

"Where did he come from?" I asked.

"His mother is a maid here"—so she was still alive, I thought—"and she came when she still carried him in her belly. She gave birth not long after she started here. He was a horrific child, deformed as you see him now."

My mind went to the memories of those I had seen in town with syphilis, stricken mad and deformed beyond belief. I was frightened of them, and Papa did his best to keep them from me. They were street beggars, women who had fallen from grace and given their bodies to men, much like the girl whom Papa had taken in the hotel. I shuddered. He was an ugly creature, for creature he was, displaying no kind of features we can reconcile to ourselves as "human". He was not thus but a monster, a thing out of Madame Shelley's poisonous little novel. My blood went cold and I felt faint.

"Forgive me," I said, "I would like to go to my room."

I was guided by Amélie. The strength of her grip hurt and left a red ring in the flesh of my arm, but the pain was comforting.

"What did you talk about?" she said. I did not mind the insolence of her question. She and I were accomplices in this prison.

I told her of the great screaming match between the Beast and La Marche; Amélie merely scoffed. "If he is not careful," she said, "there will be trouble."

"Trouble for La Marche?"

"No," she said. "Trouble for *la Bête*. La Marche has schemed for the last few years to get this castle. Like his master, he indulges in an array of vices—women as one of them, and having no women other than those in the castle, he has had to content himself with our presence. He talks about a great plan he has hatched to overthrow *la Bête*, but we have not seen him follow through with this plan. I am sure that it is one of his great brags, since he is incapable of pleasing any woman he has."

"You have been with him," I said.

"Scores of times, *mademoiselle*," she said. "Since I came here. I do my part, make him feel empowered, but I do not give him the satisfaction of my crises. Do not blush, *mademoiselle*; in ordinary circumstances, we would not talk of this, but these are not ordinary circumstances."

She was right, of course. These were by no means ordinary circumstances, and anything I had to know I had to know. It would mean my death if I did not.

"What does he say," I asked, "of his plan, I mean?"

Amélie shrugged. "He says many things. Only that he will depose the master of the castle and take his place, and rule over us all. And he will have a progeny to contend with the royals, a harem to himself—not a soul on earth can stop him, and God will not stretch out His hand to seize him."

Yes, a perverted madman, I thought. Just as I had described him when I came here. His offering of seed on my door panel, a sign of his virility. I felt sick again and asked for a glass of water. Amélie hurried and brought it to me.

I relished in the thirst I felt, and I drank it down quick. I sent her for another glass, though I drank slower this time. Had I been in the presence of alcohol, I am sure I would not have been fit to be seen or fit to speak.

I slept in relative peace that night, though when I emerged from my room to go down to breakfast, I was met with an older woman of the household, whose name was Adèle. She said, "The master bade me fetch you, *mademoiselle*."

My stomach turned to ice and I felt my body go numb. My heart hammered against the cage of my ribs, so hard I thought they would burst.

"He wishes me to bring you to the conservatory," Adèle went on, sensing my distress.

I felt tears well in my eyes as my body slowly eased, and my stomach turned normal. I took a deep breath, trying to not let my distress show and greet the master of the castle with a smile. On our way, we passed La Marche. I did not offer him a smile, though he had one for me: slow, insolent, a knowing smile, as if he and I were intimates and he knew a secret of mine, a damning, disgusting secret. I turned my head from him and walked on with my companion; I did not spare him a backward glance, knowing it was what he wanted.

He wanted to unnerve me, and I would not give him the satisfaction of knowing it was working.

The conservatory was on the other side of the castle, on the Beast's wing. I halted when I realized this, and Adèle stopped, too. She smiled encouragingly. "There is nothing to be afraid of, *mademoiselle*, I promise. I would not lead you into danger, even if the master asked it of me."

Another ally, like Amélie. I was gathering them more and more, it seemed. How many were on my side? We walked a little way further then turned left. The heads of armour squeaked in our direction as we passed.

We came to a halt at a great blue door and Adèle knocked.

"Come in," the master's voice called out.

In I went and I was greeted by the heat of a jungle, the sun beaming down on me and a room covered, festooned with plants and trees and vines of ivy. Flowers grew in abundance and on the far side, where the Beast stood, observing his growth, was a trellis of gleaming white roses. They were the largest I had ever seen, and greater than my mother's own bloom back home. They opened with a touch of her hand, sometimes, as though she had some magic touch with things that grew; and so it was with the Beast. He gently patted the tight bud of one and it sprouted to life with a peculiar magic I felt crackle in the room.

He turned to me, a new mask on. A handsome face this time, matching the blue of his eyes. I wondered if he smiled at all under it. I wanted him to smile now.

"Welcome to your sanctuary, should you ever need it," he said. "It is my gift to you."

My breath caught. He was gifting me this space all to myself. The tears started again, and I felt silly over them.

"There is more," he said. He took hold of my wrist and drew me to the doors of the balcony and opened them. The view was unlike any I had ever seen. It looked on the whole gorge and I heard the roar of water from the falls below and around me. The gentle spray tickled my cheeks as I closed my eyes and relished in the warmth of the sun. I looked down and saw it was a dizzying height. Foolish of me, I realized that no one should ever look down from great heights like that. I pulled away and sat in a chair by the rose trellis.

The Beast took my hand and patted it gently. He cursed himself for not having warned me of the height. I went to caress his cheek to comfort him. I touched the cold porcelain and drew my hand back. Shock went through me and the mask dislodged a little. His fury was unlike any I had seen mortal man contain. He roared and crashed around and tried to fasten it again.

When he was done and he turned to me, he saw that I trembled.

I was frightened of him and he knew it.

"Oh, oh Beauty," he said and threw himself on his knees in front of me. "Beauty, forgive me. I am a wretch and a villain for such behaviour. I implore your forgiveness."

Putting my hands on his shoulders, he looked up and I smiled, trying to hide the terror of the experience. I took from the trellis a rose. I cut it perfectly with the secateurs that sat on the table nearby, the pair usually used for dead-heading. I placed it in his hands and caught my thumb on a thorn. I gave a sharp exclamation and a drop of blood fell on a petal, turning it crimson.

After a while, sucking the blood from my thumb, the Beast held the rose up and gave a sigh. The petal had been stained, a stain like that of blood on a white silk shirt, then it started to run and cover the rest of the rose head. Soon, the array had turned entirely crimson.

I gasped.

The Beast turned to me. "This is a strange but powerful gift," he said. "I shall cherish it always. Your gift of this rose to me is enough. Thank you."

Without a word, he turned and left me alone. I had gifted him a scarlet rose, tainted with my blood, and he considered it fine. What he meant to do with it, I did not know. But his change, his wish for my forgiveness, it startled me in many ways.

Had Amélie lied to me about this creature?

No, that wasn't possible. Her tears when she told me what he did, that was real for me. I knew she told the truth, and I knew that I had to watch my steps. La Marche and the Beast would make powerful foes, and I had to choose my allies with care: Adèle and Amélie, they ranked as the greatest, for they declared it. The others, out of fear, may betray me.

There was a rustle in the trees on one side, the scrape of the balcony door.

I started and sat up in the chair. Standing by the balcony, wrapped in a dark cloak, his face obscured, hatted like a highwayman, was a man. I got to my feet and made to call for the servants and the Beast for help, but he was quicker, and stronger.

I whimpered and fought back until I heard the familiar, welcome voice of my beloved Adam Leroux in my ear. I burst into tears and, I think, fainted away.

IV

When I regained consciousness, my vision was blurred; the room around me spun and I felt as if I would vomit. A voice, distant but familiar and firm, spoke comfortingly to me. It was him, the Beast was leaning over me, his great hulking form blotting the rays of the sun.

"What happened?" I said.

"Adèle found you on the floor, in a dead faint. She called for me to come. We gave you some smelling salts." Indeed, there was a peculiar sting in my nostrils that lingered for a while after. "I am going to take you to your room," the Beast said at last. As though I weighed nothing at all, he scooped me into his arms and carried me like a sleeping child. I blushed, feeling his heat against my cheek as I pressed myself into his chest. What was this tenderness which was so new to him, and so very strange to me? Where was the gruffness of our first meeting, the ill-mannered creature of the card game? Where was the Beast I knew was a Beast, not the Beast I now knew had the heart of a man?

What had become of his temper, his monstrous form, the horror of his truth, so Amélie had said? They had melted away, no longer imposing, no longer relevant. He carried me to my room and laid me on my bed with all gentleness possible. He looked down on me with twinkling eyes, not the hard stare of our first meeting, nor that cruel blaze that confronted me as I spouted my accusations.

"Rest," he said. "The servants will attend you."

I thanked him graciously and tried my best for a smile. He waited by my bedside for a moment or two, as if he wanted to say something, but thought better of it. He turned and left the room.

My silence on the matter of Adam was wise, I told myself. What would the Beast think, or do, when he learned that my lover had entered the castle without his knowing of it? What would he do to the servants who had so failed him in their watchful security? He would not be cruel, I am sure, I said to myself, trying to figure him out now. He had not the courage for it, if his tender behaviour to me now was anything to go on. But his reaction to the accident with the strap of his mask shook me, to my core it rocked me; the idea that what was beneath the mask was so terrible he would murder to keep it hidden, for too true it seemed as if he would until he recovered his senses.

The incident seemed completely forgotten.

But Adam—Adam was here in the castle, wandering around, concealing himself in the guise of a highwayman. What had possessed him to come? if it was him at all, and not my over-tired brain, dreaming up visions of things I had lost, things I could never have again, memories of a life I was no longer part of.

No, that was not possible. I had felt him, I had heard him. When the maid was away, I checked my wrists for signs. Yes, a red ring rimmed my left wrist. It hurt to touch the skin, so raw had it been rubbed in the struggle. My heart hammered in my breast. Oh God! he was in the castle, come to save me! But in doing so, had condemned himself to this prison, and us to death. The Beast would never allow his presence here, to be sure my lover would be killed if he were found.

I lay in my bed, trembling all over. The maid had returned and I hid my wrist. I winced as the fabric of my sleeve brushed against the skin.

"There, there," said the maid as she had a cold compress ready. I could not deny feeling very hot, but when the cloth pressed against my skin, I felt the spasm of sudden cold overcome me. "Easy, *mademoiselle*, it is all right. Nothing here will harm you. Your temperature is rather high, so I am going to bring it down as best I can."

Like a child, I obeyed, lying still while she tended to my care. I could not help thinking that something was about to happen, and it showed on my face for my nurse said, "Are you all right, *mademoiselle*? You look distressed. Is something troubling you in your mind?"

Rather quickly, rather forcefully, I answered. "No. I am quite well. It was very warm in the conservatory; I had felt it when I first entered, but I shall recover. Please, could you open a window, and leave me be? I think I shall be better after a cool rest. I shall ring if I need anything, I promise."

I had to add "I promise", for my nurse was reluctant to leave my side. She relented, however, and I was left to my devices as soon as the door was closed. I fell asleep after a short while.

I woke to the sound of someone knocking on the door, and wondered if it might be my lover. Terror seized me. If I were to open this door and receive him, the Beast would surely find out that I had deceived him, for it was not in my nature to lie. I could not. Since I was a child, I could never manage the art of lying, the proof of my falsehood would be plain on my face. My mother would question me and I would go all to pieces. The deception would end there. If the Beast were to try the same, I would be defeated. He would kill us both. I rose from my bed and listened at the door. Adam's voice said, "*Ma chère,* pray let me in! I do not have much time. I will be spotted!"

The door was opened in an instant and he barged in and with a dramatic swish of his cloak, he closed and locked it. I stood there, wide-eyed and fearful; he stood, both hands against the door as if he strained all his weight against it, his shoulders rising and falling as he heaved great gulps of air. We were silent for a few seconds. He regained his breath then turned to me, looking at me as if regarding me—did he wonder if I was still virtuous? His eyes were cold, his stare hard. I blushed under their gaze and said, "If you are going to look at me like I am some kind of criminal, I will ask you to leave this room immediately and depart the castle for ever."

He made no answer, but pulled down the cloth over his mouth so that his face could be revealed. He was still as handsome as ever, his green eyes deep and penetrating. But his mouth was set in a hard line, grim and serious.

"Forgive my evaluation of you," he said. "I had to be sure you were not a trick. I have heard too many stories of this place, in the planning of my venture, that I have become over-cautious. My darling," he said with a different tone, softer,

47

more like the voice I knew and loved so well, "my darling, I am very glad you are safe and well. You are unharmed?"

Unharmed, I said, but not unchanged. I felt myself tremble still; the cold of the compress had taken something of my iron nerve, a quality which I prided myself on in times of distress. It had seemingly abandoned me, and with that knowledge I fell to my knees and wept.

Adam threw his arms around me and held me to his chest, so close that I felt the thud of his heart, that gentle, sweet rhythm of life and comfort, that which comforts children when they arrive in the world, the sound they must hear before they are born. I cried and cried that he was here, with me. My Adam, my beloved, was here in the castle with me. I was no longer alone; I did not need to be afraid any more.

I looked up at him through my tears and he gently stroked my cheek as he looked back. I reached up and kissed him, completely, giving myself over to the need to touch him, to have him touch me, to feel him against me, his lips on mine. The need became an urge, and the urge became a desire. He lifted me onto the bed and we stripped ourselves of clothing. The moment I lost my virginity, the moment Adam had come back to me, I felt my body start as though it were on fire. The feeling spread through my body; the motions of our lovemaking turned urgent and primal. I needed him to complete me, and the deep grunts he uttered only spurred me on to ensure we belonged to each other.

A moment or two later we were granted our climax, joined, powerful; when my crises came, it came hard. His own ejaculation was abundant, strong. We panted together as we held each other close and kissed in the bliss of our con-summated union.

How long we lay there I cannot tell; the euphoria of our connection dazed me in ways I did not think possible. The loss of my virginity did strike me as odd, however. There was little pain, not like what the other girls had taught me, the girls fortunate enough to be married to the men they loved. He was a skilled lover, and it made me give pause to think that he had done this with another woman, but such thoughts I dismissed. I was glowing with contentment, in the arms of my lover.

Then I thought of the Beast and I was afraid. He would discover my infidelity—

My infidelity, I asked myself. How could it be infidelity when he and I were not lovers, when we had not promised ourselves one another? It was absurd to think of it as such, though making love before marriage was a peculiar sin. If there was a child, he would be illegitimate; I did not care then, for my child would be the mixture of Leroux and de Longforte, two very fine families in France, none better.

Still, fear held me tight. I could not think of the Beast now without it. I would have to confront him. He would come and visit me, see if I had recovered. Again, I trembled. If he were to find me in this state, there would be bloody murder done; if he discovered my lover, he would be destroyed and consumed, like the other victims Amélie had told me of. In his rage, would we see what lay beneath that mask, whatever fearsome face he might have? Was he just a great man hiding his shame, or was he, in truth, a beast unlike any this world has ever seen?

"Get dressed," said Adam, "and I will explain all. I have found a hidden way in and out of the castle."

"Is that how you got here? Is that how you managed to find me in the conservatory?"

He nodded. He had followed my trail at a distance and when he came through the tunnel and saw the castle, he knew he needed help; he could not hope to storm the castle alone. Admiral Leroux was consulted, and deemed it hopeless. He was not a coward, but thought that a militia against the Beast would be pointless. The castle would be heavily guarded, he pointed out. "I believed him. He is an experienced soldier. But I come and find no guard whatsoever. Not on the walls, not on the battlements, none even patrolling the corridors. Only suits of armour."

My stomach turned to iron and sank into the pits of my being. Now I would be sick. I rushed to the bathroom and brought up everything I had eaten and everything I had not.

"What is the matter, *ma petite*, why do you suffer?"

"The armour," I said, once I had regained control of my stomach and its convulsions.

He was confused; what about the armour?

"The armour is enchanted!" I cried. "The whole castle is enchanted! There is magic here, magic of a kind we have only heard of in fairy tales, but I have seen it. The armour knows when someone has passed by, and I am sure it will alert him."

To be sure, there was a loud roar from somewhere deep inside the castle; a great bellow of rage, a fury that no mortal has ever dared think or dream. It shook the walls around us, dust fell from the rafters above, and small flakes of paint fell from the ceiling and littered onto my hair and skin. I brushed them away.

I knew he was coming. He knew an imposter was inside the castle and he would expend every effort to find his new quarry. He would kill, no doubt, and destroy whoever dared come into his home and use one of his women.

Adam dressed quickly and made to hide under the bed. I sprayed perfume so the scent of sex would not be smelled. The window was open too, the smell would dispense quicker than I hoped. It was almost gone when a knock came to the door; I sat myself in front of the mirror, dress open at the back, and bid whoever it was come in.

It was the Beast, of course, trailed by La Marche, whom I caught blush when he saw my bare skin facing him. I looked over my shoulder to them both and smiled as best I could.

"Forgive me," I said. "I was just trying to cool myself by the window I asked the maids to open them. I loosened the stays myself." Why did I say that? Was it not obvious that I had?

The Beast surveyed me with his hard, blue eyes, and La Marche kept staring like a wolf that slavers when his pound of flesh is spotted, flesh he is eager to sink his fangs into and taste the blood beneath.

"My guards alerted me," said the Beast, "that an intruder has entered the castle. He came in this direction and was seen coming into your room."

This is it, I said to myself. You must do all you can to protect your lover now.

"He had?" I said, incredulously. "I never saw a man enter my room. Surely, your guards are mistaken?"

His voice thundered in a growl. "My guards are never mistaken, nor do they lie."

The final word echoed in my head like it had the whole the castle.

His tone changed, for he saw me shaking. The memory of his last outburst weighed on me heavily, as it must have done him, for he said, "Forgive me, I do not mean to let my temper get the better of me."

"Nay," I said, "I am not at all familiar with this world of yours, *monsieur*. I am a woman; I do not understand these things."

A good card to play, yes. The defenceless, unknowing woman act. That usually tricked men.

"A woman you may be," he said, "but not an unintelligent one. You may not understand this place, or this world, but you know it very well. You know it to be magic."

"I had my suspicions after my first few weeks here. Perhaps I took that idea for granted."

"Perhaps, indeed. But this magic serves me, and it cannot lie to me."

La Marche tugged his master's sleeve and said, "There is a scent in here."

The Beast sniffed the air and paused for a moment. He turned angrily to his servant and said, "Damn it, La Marche, it is only the perfume she is wearing."

"No, master," said La Marche. "There is the scent of woman in the air. And man. I smell the seed of man, and the water of woman."

The creature, the disgusting creature at the Beast's side, had sniffed out my scent as a dog might. My body went rigid and I glared hard.

"How dare you, sir!" I cried with all the indignation I could muster. I wanted to see this thing punished, for his insolence of knowing the truth had made me wrathful. I turned on my stool and stood up slowly, as might a judge who is passing sentence on a condemned man. "I have never been so insulted in all my life," I went on. "You come into my room, a guest in this castle, and you accuse me of having bartered my virtues with an intruder and a villain? You forget your place, sir. And I ask that you both leave this room and leave me in peace."

The Beast seemed impressed with my outburst, my controlled words. He chuckled.

"You make a fine actress, my dear. But you do not fool the nose of La Marche, faithful dog to the Beast."

So, he already knew. He knew the identity of the intruder, he knew he was in here, and he knew what I had done.

"Where is he?" he said, the thunder returning to his voice.

I dared not speak. I feared he would strike me. I closed my eyes and hoped it would all end there, that the fatal blow would come with only a single second of pain, a sharp tearing and a blinding whiteness before I sank into oblivion and my eyes closed for ever. But there was no such moment that followed. I heard a tremendous explosion, the sound of a pistol firing, and a roar of pain.

My eyes forced open and I saw the Beast on the ground, nursing a wounded shoulder. He had been shot. My lover stood tall and proud. I have some strange image in my memory, though it cannot be possible, that he wore the trappings of a hero, his cloak billowing in the wind. He grabbed my wrist and pulled me from my seat. My open dress flapped against the bare skin of my back, the laces gently tapping me.

We passed ladies and gentlemen who were busy with their work, all of them confused, but some cried out. The heads of the armour suits snapped into life, facing the direction we ran in. This way and that, we sped down corridors unfamiliar to me. I wondered, but did not say to my lover, if we ought not to try for the entrance and plead with the coachman to take us far away, out of the Beast's reach.

Down we went now, down, down, into the bowels of the castle, through the dungeon of the Beast, where in their cells, bodies still sat, waiting for deliverance, some crouched, others huddled in corners, their heads slumped as if in sleep. They were horribly decayed. I did not want to look at them, the smell repulsed me.

"Quickly, you must trust me. We are about to pass into grotesque country," Adam said, and he opened a door.

I tried to keep from retching; my lover had led me into the bowels of a butcher's den.

Bodies were strewn here and there, some hacked to pieces and slabs of meat thrown to one side or another of the room. Blood stained the walls and the floor was the colour of copper. How long had these bodies been here? The flies were everywhere, covering every inch of them, drinking the blood, savouring the taste of slaughter.

But these poor souls had not been savaged by claws, bore no bite marks on their bodies or any such indication that they had been murdered by the Beast. The implements were human and were used by human hands.

In the corner of the room was a large pile of clothes, aristocratic and maid's wear.

I covered my mouth with my hand and we hurried through this stage set for debauchery and depraved hunger.

A little way down the corridor, turning this corner and that, we came bursting through a door into the bright light of day. I gulped the sweet-scented air of the outside world, falling to my knees, wetting my hands on the river-sprayed moss on the rocks. I cherished the feel of the dirt I touched, the roaring sound of the falls beside us. A great torrent of water to our right bordered by a drop. We had not reached the gorge bottom, but we were close.

"Come, let us away. The noise of the falls will mask the sound of someone following."

We hurried along a narrow path of stone that jutted out the edge of the rockface which then smoothed out into a wider path. On the other side of the gorge was a small opening, large enough for us to squeeze through. "On the other side is freedom," said Adam. "We are so very close!"

We squeezed through, shimmying in that tight space. I felt stricken with fear suddenly, thinking that I would not get out. The laces of my dress caught on a rock and I fell into panic, struggling to free myself and trying desperately to follow Adam to safety, to my freedom. Tears started in my eyes and streamed down my cheeks. I cried for him to not leave me. I feared that I would, in the end, be abandoned, like my father had done when he lost me, like my mother had done when she died and left me alone.

"Come, it is all right," said Adam and he unhooked my laces. "You are free. Come now, we must hurry. The coach is not too far!"

We pushed out that claustrophobic space and out into free open air. I thanked *bon Dieu* for his kindness. Running a little way further we came upon that blessed coach, the driver waiting in his seat. He was hunched over as though in sleep, and Adam called for him to wake and drive as fast as could be driven, but he did not stir. I felt that ever-present fear gnaw at my hopes once more; the coachman moved as if turning to face us. He fell from his perch and onto the ground, dead. His face was turned upward so that we saw the extent of his wounds. His throat had been slashed savagely by a knife.

"Naughty, naughty girl," said the voice of La Marche who appeared from round the other side of the carriage. "You have been very naughty indeed, and the master is not happy."

His bellow of fury echoed through the trees, and La Marche laughed to see me tremble.

"He is coming," he taunted. "He is coming for you, and he will not be merciful."

Adam drew his pistol and pointed it. He pulled the trigger, but the charge did not ignite. I stared, stunned, horrified that his best weapon failed to work. In an instant, La Marche was on him and gnashing his teeth like an animal, groping for his throat with both hands.

There was a large branch nearby which I picked up and used to strike our assailant on his back. I struck again and again till the heavy branch gave and he had recovered. He turned on me and snarled like a beast, like his master before him.

He drew a dagger and before I knew what had happened, a cravat of crimson spilled through my lover's balaclava, a spouting fountain of scarlet that seeped through his protecting fingers. I did not scream; I had neither the power or the will to do so. Blankly I stared, as my Adam's life drained out of him along with his blood. La Marche turned to me and sneered. "A good job, too," he said. "He will make a meaty morsel."

Clarity comes, at times, as though by lightning; the clarity of his truth came with a punch to my stomach. He had leaped on me and his clenched fist made contact with my unprotected belly. I wore no corset that might soften the blow. The wind was knocked out of me. He grabbed my hair and made me face him. I cried out in pain and reached for his hand which, tightening its grip, pulled harder. I felt as though he might tear my scalp from my head and take my hair as a trophy as had been done to Rapunzel.

A roar filled the trees and there was a violent crash as La Marche let go and was thrown against a nearby tree. He was winded but got up quickly. I knew he was present, I knew he was beside me, as I sprawled in the dirty, nursing my stomach which pained me greatly.

"I did nothing to you," the Beast said. "I did nothing to harm you; I gave you no reason to betray me."

"You would have, soon enough," I replied, defiantly. "Do you not think I don't know who you are? Or what your creature is up to?"

The Beast half-snarled. It was his turn to grab me by the hair and yank me up. I gave a cry and tried to grab at his wrist. La Marche taunted and jeered in the background, "Do it, sir, do it! The whore will reap what she sows!"

Again, I cried out, begging for him to stop, that I would tell him everything. I would say all I had to say, all that I knew, and who told me.

This seemed to intrigue him. "You would betray those who told you these secrets?"

"What have I to lose? There is nothing on this earth for me now. Your creature has seen to that. Look!" I pointed the body of my scarlet-garbed lover, the blood welling still from his open throat. "See your work, Beast!"

This seemed to surprise him, for his gaze turned from my lover back to me again, and in his eyes was a strange, forlorn look, a look I could only call sadness. I wanted to pity him, but I did not. I struck out with my fist and caught the side of his mask. It came away completely and shattered against a tree. The air was filled with the tinkle of porcelain shards.

His face was turned away so that I did not see it. When he faced me at last, the blood drained from my cheeks and the courage I once had turned my bowels to water. I felt a shameful trickle run down my thigh as I saw the thing in front of me.

His head was that of a bison from the new world: short, half-moon horns, enormous in shape, fur as black as night and dancing in waves on the breeze. His teeth were human and I imagined what it would be like to feel such teeth sink into my flesh. Only his eyes were the same, that strange, icy blue of our first meeting, the same blue that had blazed in rage as I accused him, that softened when we talked and when I made an offer of a blood-smeared rose. This was the face of the Beast, and a Beast he truly was.

"Now you have seen," he said. "Now you know. Now you will never be free."

A fist collided with the side of my head and I fell into the oblivion of unconsciousness.

V

When I came to, I found myself in my bed. Somewhere deep in the bowels of the castle, someone was screaming. My face hurt. He had struck the bones of my cheek, and I felt a generously large bruise had swollen there.

The wailing went on, terrible, high, a shriek for mercy that would not be given. A terrible knowledge came into my head, that someone, somewhere, in the castle was being tortured.

I sat up slowly, nursing the bruise that formed on the side of my face, trying my best to not touch it. The door opened and in came Amélie. Her face was no longer that conspiratorial mask I had known for weeks, but a mask of fury she did not deign to hide. She was furious with me, and I did not blame her. But what could I have done? the rational part of my mind said in a calm, measured way—something I found irritating, even to myself. There was no way we could have taken her with us. She would have suffered the same as Adam.

Adam...

The memory came surging back and I involuntarily burst into tears. I covered my face with my hands and wept. Amélie said nothing, but watched me, silent, grave. After a while she found her voice, cold and cruel. "Weep all you want," she said. "It makes no different. It will not bring him back. There is no-one left to weep for Adèle, they are all too frightened. She is marked a traitor. She is being punished for your crime."

Oh God, not Adèle. Why did he choose her, of all people? Why did he have to make an example of the woman who was so motherly, so sweet, who bucked the girls up and gave them the courage they needed to continue? What cruelty had possessed him to punish her?

"Where are they?" I demanded. "Where have they taken her?"

"The master has taken her to his chambers," she said.

I fell back against my pillows and stared into nothing, thinking of the poor woman and the tortures being administered. Again, I heard from far away the cries of that good, gentle soul; I resolved to put an end to it. If anyone was to suffer, then let it be me.

"Get a dress ready for me," I said, firmly, taking on the tones of a commander of soldiers ready to go into battle. Amélie stared at me for a moment.

"What do you want a dress for?"

I did not give her my plan, for I did not know it then myself. What did I purpose to do to the Beast when I reached his chamber? Would I fight him, would I reason with him? I would have no help from the servants, they were all too afraid to go near the place, and with the sounds that came from his chambers, they would have run from their work and hid in their quarters in the underbelly of the castle.

"Get me the red gown from the cupboard, and make me like a rose," I said. "Don't argue; just do as I say." My battles had made me bold, for Amélie stared now with incredulity, but she went about her task with as much quickness as one could expect. She dressed me in the finery of my station, this dress of scarlet velvet, furled and shaped like the petal of a rose, and with the roses of his conservatory in mind, with the gift I had given him of flower and blood, I covered the bruises with makeup, smeared my lips with crimson lip paint, and would march to his door and enter.

What I planned to do next was unclear, but I would confront him. If anyone deserved to be tortured, it was me. I would demand he let Adèle go and take me in her place. It was my doing that had brought such misery to this castle and its occupants, what more harm would be given if I were to be destroyed in her stead? I thought then of what Amélie said of his consuming his staff. But the bodies in the butcher's den did not seem done as by an animal with claws and teeth, for no such signs of violence was there. I saw a puncture in one, a thin red line with a trickle of blood.

It clattered in my brain at last. The final piece of the puzzle of downstairs' monstrous exhibition had slotted into place; the Beast was not killing these girls, or eating them at all.

What had killed that poor creature was the wound from a knife.

The butchering that followed, the desecration to come, could only have been undertaken by a human hand.

I felt faint once more as Amélie tried to apply the eyeshadow.

I told her my realization, and the blood went from her face. Then that face hardened to its mask once more and she said, "And what about the blood and clothes, in the master's room? Where do they come from?"

"They are their clothes, but he must strip them of their garments and deal with them in some way we don't understand. There must be passages into his chambers, secret ones, which lead to the kitchen, should he not wish to take dinner below?"

Amélie thought for a moment, then the light broke on her.

"The Beast must leave, and La Marche deals with them. He kills them and gives orders that the room be cleaned before the master returns."

"But we have seen the blood," said Amélie.

"Yes, you have," I said. "But who told you that the Beast consumes those whom he asks to his rooms?"

Amélie did not answer for a while, the blood had drained from her face once more. She looked like a woman who did not know how much more she could take. "La Marche," she said. "He told it to me when he bragged of his plan to kill the master, and take his place as owner of the castle. He said it was his right to have, since he had served him for so long. He said that he would no longer serve a cannibal master."

"He deceived you," I said. "He deceived us all. The Beast has done no wrong in such a way as to kill and consume. Indeed, he is guilty of nothing!"

"How can you say so, when he has treated us women so abominably?"

"Yes, he has. He has taken us from homes and loving families. I can't understand why, but I think I know his reasons. His mother. He loved her so, and wished to treasure her. He did treasure her. Now he wishes to fill his house with all these women so he can feel closer to her."

"It is not sound reasoning," said Amélie.

"There is nothing sound about this place," I retorted. "It is a castle of deception, a castle of murder, filled with the scent of blood. It is no longer a place in which anyone can live."

"And what can we do to change that?"

I did not answer and left her waiting for one. I did not think it possible that it could be changed. It had gone on for so long, longer than we could possibly imagine. And La Marche, I knew, had tainted this place with his depravity, had plastered the roots of this castle with blood, innocent blood he had on his hands. I wondered, too, if the Beast was aware of it. Would I take another stand, like I had in my first week, and put to him the actions of another? I wondered if he would see my words and what they meant, or if he would be so taken with rage that he would never listen.

I was ready, the gown swathed around me, hugging tight against my breast.

Beautiful, I thought. I looked beautiful; I looked ready to confront a monster.

Out in the corridor, I was greeted by the pale, angry, scared faces of the maids who stood outside my door. They all stared at me with wide eyes. I shuddered, for they frightened me now, not saying a word. Tears stained their cheeks. For a moment I thought I would wilt, like the flower I had gone to such lengths to make myself, but found in me a great surge of courage. I would hold my head high and walk towards the Beast's wing of the castle.

I said, "You can stand and stare as long as you please. I am going to the master's room. I do not know the way, and would wish very much for one of you to kindly guide me there."

Not one of them spoke, not one of them moved.

Amélie appeared behind me and said with a whisper in my ear, "I will take you."

I did not need to thank her; she saw it already, in my face.

The maids around the door parted and made a lane for us. We walked between them, I felt their eyes all on me, following as I passed them. Whispers hissed behind me, though I did not catch what was said. I didn't want to.

The girls did not follow us, their fear was too much, and they dispersed when we two turned a corner towards the other side of the castle.

I had not thought the way so long, but it felt like a lifetime before we came to the lobby, where I had first taken the steps to my new destiny, shedding the skins of my old life. I looked down on that room, at the tables lined with ornaments, at the great Persian rug on the floor, of the great circle of light that came from above, the glistening shards of colour dancing below. I thought, curiously, that I would never see it again after this adventure, that it was a pleasure to be indulged for a last time before I met whatever end awaited me.

Amélie tugged on my arm to break me from my reverie and we walked on.

Now, we had come to the Beast's wing of the castle. It was a mess, not like what it had been some hours ago. Suits of armour had been thrown across the corridor and pieces which had come loose were strewn across the scarlet carpet. The magic of the castle had attempted, in some curious way, to piece them together, but they made only grotesque mockeries of what they once were. Deformed and hateful, like their master's stooge.

I am surprised that I do not think of the Beast as such; deformed and twisted though he was, he had not the sinister feeling he had had when we met, when he had proposed to my father that game of cards. That had all gone. In his place was a creature I pitied, a creature who had known the love of a mother and who begged for it again. His pathetic display in the conservatory had shaken me still. His words rang still in my ears, "Oh Beauty, Beauty! I am wretch and a villain for such behaviour!" Which part of me wanted to believe his words? Did I want to believe his tale, of kindness and generosity as a child, only to lose it all under the reign of a father who neither loved him or cared?

This conflict, so fierce, so eager to take hold now, as I walked towards his chambers, set my soul to wonder, and from wonder to doubt.

At last we reached the door of his domain. Amélie said, "I cannot interfere; this is now your fight. I will not come in. I will not wait. But I will give you the courtesy of knocking."

I thanked her and bade her flee before his wrath turned to her.

She knocked and sped down the passage.

For that moment I was alone in front of his door, I wondered if he heard—if they both had, to be sure his faithful servant would be present, watching as the poor woman cried out for mercy.

There it was, so close, so frightened, freezing the blood in my veins, a ghostly, painful wail of desperation and despair.

I knocked hard on the door. They had not heard the first time. One, two, three times I beat my fist against the panel.

There was a loud scuffle from within, a roar of anger, and the thunderous footsteps of the Beast approaching. The door wrenched open and the bison's head was thrust out. He made to snarl and curse but when he saw me, he stopped. His eyes widened. He did not expect me, it was obvious. Now, I stood before him, unafraid yet trembling.

"What do you want?" he said. His voice had softened, but his eyes had not.

"I have come to talk, and remove the woman you have in there, Adèle."

He did not respond. I stepped forward, emboldened by our battles, attempting to be as fierce as possible, and I was so close to his face, I could smell the animal scent of musk in his fur. "She had nothing to do with what I have done, and she is not deserving of the punishment you are giving her. Let her go. And take me instead."

The Beast lifted his head and smiled a peculiar kind of smile. The smile of a demon.

"I will let her go," he said. "And I will invite you in."

He opened the door wider and allowed me entry. I stepped into his domain and found it a mess, like the halls outside. Strewn with litter and torn clothes, the bedclothes too were on the floor and ripped to shreds. Some of them even had stains of blood. At the far end, where a light fell on her like a light from heaven, Adèle was strapped to a wooden chair, beaten and as bruised as I was. A great purple mark had swollen across her face and disfigured her. I could not help but gasp.

I ran to her side and tried to get the straps undone. La Marche caught me by the throat and threw me to the side. He was armed with a dagger; he drew it now.

"Enough!" the Beast cried. "She is not to be harmed, and nor is the woman in the chair, is that understood?"

La Marche, reluctant, but sneering at me all the same as though he were not done with his fun yet, said, "Yes, master." He sheathed his dagger and with a long, pale, tongue licked his lips.

I got back to the straps and let Adèle go. She sat dazed and confused, like she had been drugged, her head lolling from side to side on her shoulders, unable to focus on anything.

"What have you done to her?"

A sleeping powder, the Beast said, administered to her in a vulnerable moment, so that she did not panic.

I let her wrists free, and her feet. The cords had bitten into her skin, rubbing them till they bled. The good woman whimpered as I set her free, delirious, knowing not where she was or what was happening to her.

I turned to the Beast and said, "Am I to believe that you are better, than this?" I did not expect him to answer, nor did I wish him to, not till I had finished. "What would your mother think if she could see you now? What would she do?"

The Beast's eyes narrowed and his great head lowered close to mine. "My mother made me this creature, as punishment."

"And perhaps she was right to do so," I said. Another blow to the back of my head from La Marche, and I was silenced. I cried out, and felt the world around me go blurry. The Beast roared.

"No more, I said!"

"You kill your maids, you kill them!" I cried and the world was quiet. "You, the Beast, you kill your staff when you summon them here and you eat them!"

I looked up and saw his eyes meet mine, they were wide with horror. "What did you say to me?" he said, the beginnings of rage in his voice.

"You eat your women, kill them, butcher them. I have seen them, deep in the castle, in the dungeon. It is a carving den there, where the bodies of all the women you have loved and used are stored, and you shall eat them. Is that the food you bade me eat at your table? Is that what life you have given me? How many have been consumed by you, how many?" I cried, and the great gloved hand wrapped round my throat, so powerful that a gentle squeeze would snap my neck and it would be over. I would slip from his grip and fall to the floor in an indecorous heap.

"I have done nothing to these women," he snarled. "Nothing. I have only given them a home and a better life."

"There is no life, living on the edges of a menu," I said between gasps. "You think that I lie, sir? Go to your dungeon, the path I took with my Adam, and you will find the butcher's den. I know where you have carved you meals up."

The Beast threw me aside onto the bed and he thundered from the room with a great bellow of rage.

My plan had worked, he was enraged and would see the truth of his servant. But I did not account for being left alone with that servant, the most dangerous creature in the castle.

He stared at me, standing beside Adèle and smirking. A gleam of teeth showed beneath those thin lips, strong, capable of tearing flesh from bone. I trembled, but made every effort to not let him see that I did.

"You are very clever," he said, "to have stumbled on the den. I was sure that no-one would have gone there, nor would they have found it."

"My Adam had, when he gained entry into the castle. He passed through and got to the dungeons. I thought that Amélie's words were truth, that he did eat the women of his castle. It fit his temperament as a beast, did it not? But no, you spread the rumour of your own depravity and put it on an innocent."

His smile broadened; his teeth looked very strong, very sharp.

"I notice that you do not say 'man'."

"He is not a man, and he knows that well."

"Not now, he is not. And he never will be again. Not like in those fairy tales your mamas and papas told you when they tucked you in at night. This is the reality. He is the Beast."

From below, like before, the walls danced to the tune of his great, furious roar. Pictures jittered and rattled, dust fell from the rafters and flakes of plaster and paint fell onto my head.

At last! my mind screamed with triumph; at last, he knows! He will be here soon, and he will deal with his servant.

But La Marche smiled still, his triumph secure that he had tricked his master and shamed him. "He may know now," said La Marche, "but he will never forget his shame. And I will have this castle."

He drew from his back a pistol, ready and loaded. I crept up the bed, fearful that he was going to shoot me. He laughed. "Fret not," he said. "This is not for you." He grinned. "But I do have something that is," he said. "A parting gift, you could say."

It happened very fast, though I remember every moment of it. What woman forgets the moment of her violation? He was on me in an instant, like a predator that has pounced, and he struck me, again and again, till I gave in and could fight no more. He unfastened his britches and I felt his sudden penetration. It hurt. Feebly I tried to kick out or hit him with my fists, but it did not help. He only thrust more eagerly if I struggled, and pinned my wrists above my head.

He was soon finished; when he was, he grunted his satisfaction and let his seed fill me—I had not the power to stop it, though I tried. When I felt him climax, tears rolled down my cheeks. I stared into space and lay there, defiled.

"A parting gift, I said, yes?" said La Marche as he fastened his britches again, looking down at me. I looked at him and saw Adèle had got to her feet, though she teetered. She had a long heavy instrument in her hands which she lifted above her head and brought crashing down on his scalp.

La Marche cried out and swore. He turned to Adèle, thrust himself forward, and fastened his hands around her throat. There was a struggle, they were throwing each other around the room in this dance between murderer and victim. I slid from the bed and grabbed the lead pole she had used to strike him. I came up behind him and I struck him again. This time he was on the floor. I took the pistol from him and stood, taking aim.

He got up from Adèle, crouching over her body, for she was dead. I was not quick enough to save her. But I would save everyone else in this castle. I pulled back the hammer, pointed it at his head and waited.

There was an explosion of sound as the Beast returned from his excursion. He saw the body of Adèle, saw La Marche standing over her and he snarled. "No more!" he cried. I turned away when I saw the Beast leap. La Marche screamed as he was torn to pieces, and I heard the flesh tear and squelch. The gurgling sound he made in his throat as he died has never left me. I shall hear it always.

When it was over, and I opened my eyes to look, the Beast was standing over the corpses and panting heavily. He said nothing to me; he didn't need to. He turned to face me, his black fur matted with blood, his eyes wide with horror, for he had committed a barbarous act. This, the first and only creature he had destroyed, his servant, and he was glad to have done it.

"You found the lair?" I asked. A stupid question, but I could find no other words to say.

"Yes," he said. "I found it. And I nursed such evil in my home, I let it run free and did not think anything of it."

"He planned to kill you, today," I said.

I told him what Amélie told me, of his brags when they shared a bed. He made to find her but I stopped him. She was no part of his plot; he had been sleeping with many maids, using them as he saw fit. And through that, he talked and spread the rumours of the Beast's monstrous appetites.

"I did not realize until I saw a mark on one of the bodies: a mark made by a knife."

He sighed and sat on his bed. The rush of excitement had died down. Now I felt sore, I clutched my belly and fell to my knees. The Beast loomed over me and placed me on the bed. How could I keep that from him? I told him of my violation, too. His fury, his rage, had not been spent yet. He went to the body of his fallen servant, gathered it up and threw it from his balcony, a trail of blood trickled behind him.

"Let this be an end to this violence and suffering," he said.

He approached and grabbed the pistol from my hand, turning it in his. He said nothing. I knew what he purposed to do, but did nothing to stop him.

He went to the window and stepped out onto the balcony. I followed, so he did not have to be alone. He put the barrel of the gun to his head, clicked back the hammer once again, and shot himself. A violent, jerking convulsion went through him as the charge exploded and blood sprayed over the balcony ledge. I clapped my hands over my mouth. He teetered for a moment on the edge, leaned back, and was lost over the rail and down to the frothing chasm a few hundred feet below.

I stared for some seconds, then turned from where he had fallen. I saw on the floor, by the chair, the rose I had given him, the rose stained with my blood. My chin wobbled with the beginning of tears. What had happened, what had I done? What had he done? I burst into tears then and picked the rose up from the floor. I turned it in my hands and surveyed it. Once pearly white, now crimson with the spread stain of my blood, I stroked the silken petals. A moment or two passed, when the crimson started to fade.

Each petal lost its colour, like blood draining from a dead face. What manner of magic it was, I don't know; there was nothing splendid about it, nothing great or dramatic, a magician could have conjured it. But it drained away, and the blood crept over my hands.

I dropped the rose then and watched the scarlet red rivulets converge on a spot on my finger, the point where the thorn had pricked me. Each trickle moved in unison, eager to at last converge on that point—a gift received from me, a gift given back.

The master was dead; there was no use for my gift any more.

For a moment or two I stood astounded, the blood sank into my skin again. A warmth passed through me, like a warm breath on the back of my neck, inviting, welcome. It was at that moment that the castle started to tremble.

VI

We live at home, quiet and confined, so says Anne Elliot in that wonderful novel, *Persuasion*. I think it is the best way to describe our circumstances, Amélie and mine, since there is no longer a castle to speak of.

It trembled like a live thing when its master was discovered dead; the magic that kept it standing had no further use, and whatever pact had been made with nature to make it had come to an end. It had no purpose now; it was no longer needed. The Beast was dead; the staff at last had their freedom, the freedom they had dreamt of for so long.

Some of them had had no revelation that they are free, they stayed at their posts and would not move.

I cannot imagine what it must have been like, to have been so frightened of their master that they would rather die at their post than risk it all to live a little longer. Most of us made it out, though there is not much I can say for those whose souls lay in that place.

There was a great clamour and a crash as the carved walls of the castle started to crack and lines, as jagged as lightning, ran up the face of them.

Windows shattered and showered us with glass; the relics inside could not be saved, no matter what treasure they might be. I grieved at the loss of the paintings, especially that of Jove and Leida, what a fine thing that would be to possess!

Lost to the chasm, like my friend, like his castle.

Amélie and I found one another not long after the castle crumbled. Upon meeting, we embraced each other warmly. We shared tears, too. I told her all that had happened, and what the Beast had done. Her reaction was what I had expected, incredulity and more tears.

Life has changed for us a good deal. Those who worked in the castle have moved on to have families of their own, while they have the chance. They have married and kept close to one another. I am glad of that. It would be sorrowful indeed if they were to forget one another after all they had done and been through. I think that of Amélie. She stays with me, now; and we live peacefully away from society, away from prying eyes who know our names, who know mine. I have not told my father of our release, and I don't intend to. I do not wish to bother or remind him of his folly.

Let him live his life in peace, away from each other, away from my cold tongue and my harsh words. I enjoy my present peace, though I fear something will come along to wreck it. To my surprise, it has not happened on us yet. Is it an unnecessary anxiety, brought on by the trauma experienced in that place? Or is it something else, a gift of premonition granted me by the gift of my blood from his rose?

A queer thought, I know; but whatever the Beast possessed, I must assume was imbibed with magic. It could perhaps be my womanly intuition, a gift some men are granted and others are not.

I will not let it bother me, not today, even as I write.

I cannot lie and say that it has been a smooth transition. There are plenty nightmares shared by myself and my companion. When we wake, we talk about them. This is helpful, since I have no-one else to whom I can speak. Being with someone who understands, someone who knows, is the most liberating thing in the world.

After some weeks, almost a month, when things started to right themselves, I began to feel ill. In the morning I would be sick and Amélie would rub my back tenderly, a comforting presence as I knelt in the water-closet, vulnerable and shaking.

When I realized I was with child, I wondered what I ought to do. Should I kill the thing growing inside me, praying it would not be like his infernal father who defiled me? Or ought I to let it live, and hope it was like the man I loved so dearly, who had shared my bed first? The dilemma tore me in many directions. I wanted to love the child, since he would be a gift, but thoughts of La Marche haunted me; I prayed he would be nothing like him. If he was, I fear I might have smothered him in the night and be hanged for a barbarous murder.

Little Pierre was born and I was presented with him. I smiled and cried. He was a bonny thing, so very handsome that I could have died. Then he opened his eyes and I felt myself grow weak. He had the eyes of his father.

He has grown into a little prodigy, eager to learn opera and play the pianoforte.

What pleasure he brings us; to think I thought of killing him…

He will sit with us, and I will read to him, and Amélie will sit on the other sofa and she will listen, smiling as I read. We are halfway through *Robinson Crusoe* now, which has become a very quick favourite, more than *Gulliver's Travels* had.

I love those times when we just sit and I read aloud. He loves it, too. He asked me every night to read him a bed time story, saying "You have a lovely voice, Maman." I can't help but be flattered and will tell him a fairy tale, about a strange castle in a gorge not too far from here, and I will tell him of its occupant who was as strange as his home, for he was no ordinary man, but a creature cursed and in search of love and rescue.

The usual question came at the end. "Why don't you write this down? It ought to make a very fine novel."

I thought about that to. It would make a fine novel, but I did not have the skill to make it thus. I tell him that every time, and he pouts. "Maman, you tell beautiful stories," he says. "I would read them all the time!"

I kiss him, tuck him in, and leave one candle burning on his bedside table.

When we were alone in the drawing room of our cottage, and Amélie was darning one of Pierre's stockings, I brought the matter up.

"Pierre thinks I ought to write down the version of our story I tell him as a novel. A fairy tale, of sorts."

Amélie did not answer at first. She went on darning his stocking.

"I do not know. I feel it might help exorcise the ghosts we feel still. Every shadow in our path, every corner in this cottage we turn, we are so cautious, as if we expect to find ourselves in his hands again."

Amélie stopped sewing. She looked up and glared at me.

73

"What do you expect, when we have seen horror? Is that not what happens? Is that not the same as when men come home from war, greatly changed? You do whatever you must to get it out of your head, in any way you think right. But do it. And if the world must know, then let the world know. I will not stop you."

"But you will not help me, either," I said. It was stated as a fact, not a reproach. She had made it clear she would not help, even if she was pleaded with. No, the memories were not to be borne, not again. Not even for Pierre.

To twist them was to trivialize it all, to play games and tell lies about it. And lies, Amélie said, was not what she was about.

"Pierre will never know the truth," I said. "Not until he is older, not until we are gone; I can write two accounts, one for him to be comforted by. The other to tell him the truth when he is older, when he will understand."

The suggestion did not soothe her; I did not expect it to. I hold no expectations with my friend, not any more. But I feel she expects a good deal from me, in areas of life and matters I am not prepared to tell my son. When he is asleep, when we are alone, we can talk. But we never talk about the castle, we never talk about the Beast…

"Perhaps it is time we talked about it," I said at last. "We keep silent about it for so long, we pretend like it did not happen, but it did. Why do we pretend, what use is there?"

She finally threw her stockings down and glared at me hard. Her voice was harsh, cold.

"I pretend because I want to believe there is some kind of life for me after that infernal place; I want to pretend that life can continue as normal, that we can sit at a table, eat our meals, and I can be an aunt and godmother to your child, as you bade me be when he was born. I wish to live in peace, to live unmolested by those memories, by the nightmares. I do not wish to read of it, nor do I wish to hear of it. I wish to forget."

"Then help me forget, when I write it."

She softened then, looked into my eyes, and started to cry.

I have begun my fictional account. It is called "The Tale of the Beauty and the Beast."

I like the title, though I find it a little egotistical. I have had my share of beauty, though it has been marred somewhat after my experiences. I do not care. Life has begun again for me, and I do not intend to let it go.

Amid these pages, I spend most time, for this is an account for my son. When I die, I will leave him the truth, which he deserves. He is too young now to understand what he is, or where he comes from. But he deserves the name of his father.

My tale progresses in its novel form, though my true account has come to an end. This is perfect for the ground work I wish to establish in my new tale, the tale he will read when it is done—a tale, perhaps, many others will tell their children, and read to them when they are put to bed.

I like to think of such things, mothers telling their children about a magic castle in some hidden part of France, where they can always find beauty, even if they must confront the beast who guards it. The rose must have prime place, too. I cannot forget the rose. I kept it, still, in a small album of drawings.

My mind does not let me forget the images of that castle, so I have decided to illustrate it—perhaps it will be good for the novel? I am no master artist, though I do admit to some skill.

But at night, I will sit with my son, take out the pages I have written on and I will read it to him. He will be entranced, and he will be given the images of his father. And I am there in the story with him, walking the castle corridors, smiling on the maids who were at work, and there will be his father, his father who stands on the balcony on which he died, a new mask to cover his face, one that smiles at last. He will take it off and his great, bison's head will be held high, and he will smile. I will stand with him, and my Adam will stand by my side, too. We are friends, together in my realm of magic.

The Devil's Pit

The Devil's Pit

The expedition was not meant to be complicated but was made so by their guides' refusal to go anywhere near the place they were looking for.

They arrived in Brazil two days before and arrangements were made by locals who could be trusted and a group of men were found who would take them to "the Devil's Pit". No-one would tell them why it was named thus, or what was inside. But, said Armstrong, that was why they were there: explorers were meant to discover things, and they would discover the truth of that unmarked valley.

The three of them had come straight from those hallowed halls of learning, Oxford and Cambridge, and after they graduated with flying colours (if not for the pay-offs and cajoling of some third party members who would write their essays for them and tutor to them, in simple terms, what they had to do) the thought of adventure excited them. They spent their early years cooped like uneasy pigeons in big houses with wide lawns and parks of many acres, preferring to be outside and exploring the woods, playing cowboys and Indians, pretending to be great explorers who had discovered the source of the Nile or the City of Gold deep in the jungle. After their graduation, the Amazon seemed the best way to initiate themselves into the realms of science and discovery they often daydreamed of.

There were three from England who had come to Land of Jaguar: Armstrong, tall, fair, and ruggedly handsome, with little brain and the famous opinion that Anglo-Saxon men would determine the fate of the world, for Queen and empire was the way to go. Johnson, the second, was smaller, darker, with little opinion of his own until one was given him. It was only when matters of an occult nature—talk of God and the Devil—was brought up that he spoke his piece and expected everyone to share it, and when they did not his feelings were beyond hurt. He would lash out and defend his faith to the death it seemed. And last of all was Denny, the most unusual and incongruous of them. Small, slight, not very strong but with a brilliant mind when it came to the natural world. He had studied biology in Cambridge and felt that the Amazon was more than welcoming.

It was he who had prepared sensibly for their journey, though the others thought that all they needed were guns and nets and boxes and boxes of ammunition; Denny would not let the clot-heads get in the way of his grand adventure. He had been waiting for this kind of opportunity all his life and here it was now, happening.

As far as arguing with the natives as to the arrangement of their guide could be called "happening".

When they docked and caught their first glimpse of this exotic land they were struck immediately by the oppressive heat, having noticed the change when they passed over the equator on the Atlantic voyage. The heat assaulted them as vigorously as any of the sights and smells and colours of any foreign land that wasn't England. The three men, being little versed in the etiquette of one who visits a different country, understood little of what went on. Their roughness was unpardonable and their manners (if they could be called such) were much worse. Nothing pleased them if it was not going their way, and invariably the wrong way was how it went. When they reached their rendezvous, things appeared to have escalated.

Men would talk of demons, others of monsters; some would pretend (and the gentlemen knew they pretended) to have never heard of the place. It was farcical, the fine men thought; they had learned everything they could find on the place, and they were so close now. Why would they risk their necks on something mystical when it had been talked of so widely?

The natives shrugged their shoulders. It was none of their business why the white men would waste their money looking for something that did not exist. They did it often enough, so the natives did not at all mind.

This raised some comments from both sides about empire and injustice—all of which flared the tempers of the two proud men and sent Denny ducking for cover.

After a few days' asking round, they found someone who would talk for a price. An old woman in dark robes with bands and beads that dangled from every part of her. She usually wouldn't speak of it; it was told that bad luck would follow if they did. "I am protected," she said, indicating her woven spells hanging from her roof and her person. "I can speak now."

The stories she told were horrific.

Now we know rumour and speculation are powerful things, and dangerous when one knows how to use them. But use them the old woman did not. All she spoke of was fear, a real fear that spilled from that place, and the reluctance of anyone to go near it, a reluctance well-founded, she said. Stories had come from all around that men who went in either returned greatly altered or did return at all. She would not say how or why. Bodies there were that had come from there, found on the lip of the valley, like they had been discarded by something, or left as a warning. Descriptions of mutilations, the final words from unhappy victims, earned the place its name: "The Devil's Pit". As they listened, the explorers' blood ran cold, though they afterwards felt silly, stupid even.

"And where will we find someone willing to take us there?" asked Armstrong, growing impatient with the old woman's twaddle.

She looked at him with narrowed eyes. Denny took care to remember her face: her caramel skin had the texture of a wrinkled apple, and eyes bright and fierce.

She knew what she was about, had lived long enough to see the rise and fall of warriors and leaders, had lived to see change in the world, and she looked weary of it all. But there was in her manner an alertness that never faded, a guard which was never relaxed. Denny thought that this must be the way one survives in the wild, for to be sure she had seen her share of close-calls with animals of a most perilous kind. Jaguars, snakes, those awful bird-catching spiders—she must have seen them all and bore many scars. After considering their leader, she smiled—the wry smile of someone plotting.

"My son will take you," she said. "He is a good boy and will take you where you must go."

"Excellent," said Armstrong as he rose from his chair.

"But know this," she added, harsh as an old town raven. "There is nothing to stop him from running away and leaving you three to die. But he will not do that: he is not that kind of man. But do not expect him to hold true when nearing a place with much evil deep in it, from which you might never come back. We are a civilized people,' she added with an edge to her voice, "we want you British to know that."

When they left it was raining hard; a mist from the jungle seeped through the town and the rain battered down on huts and houses, hammering like fists. It did not give any relief from the heat, for this rain was hot as hell.

When midday of next came, there was a knock on their door and a handsome young man with caramel skin and stubbly face entered the room.

There was a scar that ran up the right side of his neck. He announced himself as Antonio, the son of the wise woman with whom they talked. He said that he would take them as close to the valley as he could, but could make no promises to join them entering it. The price was agreed but he would take no penny of it now. "It would be bad form to do so," he said. "That is not how gentlemen behave, is it?"

What a strange boy, they thought. Though he could not have been any younger than themselves—he must have been Denny's age at least. They sat with a map and discussed in detail the best way to go. Denny noticed that it had been marked on the map as not too far from where they were now.

"It should not take more than four days," said Antonio. "Nothing that the gentlemen are not used to, I hope."

Armstrong said, "We have spent many summers hiking and walking in the Lake District, I am sure this will be no different."

"No different in distance, I am sure," said Antonio, "but I do not think that the Lake District has the dangers that live here. The jaguar who hunts nightly; the anaconda who seeks to embrace and devour you; the spider who drops from heights above to attack whatever it can find. I am unsure if the Lake District has such dangers," he went on insolently, "but I am sure that for the courageous gentlemen it will prove easy."

There was little discussion after this, though in private Armstrong threatened to dock pay if he were ever insolent again. Antonio did not try to be humorous with them after that.

Denny, after hearing the stories of jaguars, anacondas, and bird-eating spiders made the sensible decision to write his will before he went aboard the ship to Brazil. He left everything to the care of his mother.

He was a smothering boy and not too clever when it came to people. There was talk among his mother's friends and his mother herself that it would perhaps be better if the boy got lost in the jungle, or if he would fall prey to a jaguar or a spider bite.

The boy's father left a hefty estate and fortune, and on his death the boy inherited the lot. Now that he was twenty-five, he had come into that inheritance, and his mother—charming, darling creature that she was—was living on his charity.

She took control of his estate since he had not a head for finance (his proficiency for mathematics was absurdly poor) and was happy to do so. Now he was in the Amazon, watching the rain as it burst in torrents on them, dripping through the thatch roofs, and watching the mist roll in when the deluge would end, waiting for the sun to come out in all her blazing glory.

Books were no comparison to the reality of the jungle. The sights, the smells, the colours and textures, all so different to the soft, watery shades of Britain and its forests, its rolling hills, its damp little hamlets.

The company made ready to leave, for today was the beginning of their great adventure. Antonio said goodbye to his mother, pecking her on the cheek. She looked on them all severely as they made their way into the foliage, turning away when she saw them disappear into the wall of green. She prayed for the safe return of her son, but curiously left the others absent from her plea.

How thrilling, how exciting it was to finally be on their way! Tramping into the heart of the jungle towards the most intriguing parts in the world. They would find the valley, nestle into its womb, and penetrate its heart with a marker claiming it for the British Isles. In that valley were riches beyond imagining, the discovery of a lifetime. They would be hailed as heroes when they returned home, and would be written about in *The Boy's Own Paper*. "Smashing for us, eh chaps?"

"And very deserving of it you are, too," said Johnson with the air of a lacky who cannot help but compliment their superior every chance they got.

"Do you think *you* will write about us?" Armstrong asked Denny, who, as always, trailed on the end of the line with his head down, a habit from school he found hard to break.

Denny looked up, his thin frame sweating under the heat of the sun, with a pock-marked face that never really healed, blushed to be addressed by the unquestioned leader of the group.

"I suppose I will," he said, "though I don't know what good it will do the Royal Zoological Society."

Armstrong barked a laugh.

"Has bugger all to do with the Royal Zoological Society," he said, "it's about getting us in the papers, making our names. Writing a story that will have us penetrate the heart of this virgin jungle, spreading the seed of civilization, teaching the savages what they need to know as noble, God-fearing citizens. A story that will show us discovering what no man has found before, and snatching at some glory at last. Making our ancestors proud."

As he spoke, Johnson's face lit up with admiration and love, hanging on his every word. It was impossible not to think of a small begging dog, spellbound by adoration.

Denny said, "Is there much left here that need such lessons? The people fear God enough as it is, I think."

Armstrong thought for a moment and said, "Yes, that's very true. Full of bloody Catholics this place, isn't it?" Johnson spat on the ground and muttered something about "papal bastards". Then Denny said the worst thing he could possibly say: he said that they did not need to discover the valley, since it had been discovered already. The only thing they didn't know was what was inside. This led to a heated argument amongst the three men, and Antonio only looked on as his wards battled it out with their words, only getting involved when he felt the situation escalating to the point it might come to blows.

"All I was saying," said Denny afterward, "was that we don't know what is in the valley. It could be a predator that doesn't like to be disturbed."

He hadn't enjoyed the stories he'd heard in Oxford; tales of cannibals, and snakes that could swallow a man whole. He tried his best to not think of any of it, but it didn't work.

Armstrong heard his talk with the guide and laughed. "The only predator that need be feared here now is us, Mr. Denny. Human kind."

Denny lowered his head and sighed. When he looked up, he saw Antonio, his caramel-skin glistening with sweat as the sun shone on them through the canopies above, his handsome face fiercely beautiful, his chestnut eyes glaring hard at Armstrong and Johnson. Denny thought he saw the young man's jaw tighten, as though he clenched his teeth together very hard, and he saw, too, he had a clenched fist round the hilt of his machete, the long blade stained the colour of tobacco spit.

The second day passed and Antonio said it would be wise to stop and rest. They found a glade as night fell and set up camp, cooked their meal, and gathered round the fire under an inky-blue night pricked over with a million stars.

Antonio told them the stories of ancient heroes with the powers and weapons strong enough to topple the gods; he spoke of Quetzalcoatl, the winged serpent of the jungle, whom the Aztecs of ancient days worshipped as a god, and he made mention of the first explorers who came across a great wall. When they came to the end of it, they beheld the head of a giant anaconda.

Such stories, borne of nightmares, appeared to still have the power to chill the blood in the listeners' veins, and Denny listened with awe and wonder and fear while Armstrong and Johnson sat together sniggered throughout, which their guide ignored.

It seemed Antonio was fix on Denny alone, and Denny listened as if entranced, leaning in when Antonio leaned toward him, like conspirators about to embark on a great deed.

When each tale came to its end there was a stunned silence, which Armstrong frequently broke, shattering the illusion, much to Denny's irritation.

"You don't *really* believe this twaddle, do you?"

Antonio said frankly, "It is the history of our people. We do our best to respect it. Did not the British believe in dragons and fairies, once upon a time? Or in the spirits of the earth, as our brothers in the north believe?"

Armstrong made no answer.

"And what about the valley," said Denny, eager to have the rest of it told him. "What stories are there of the Devil's Pit?"

It was Johnson's turn to be irritated.

"Oh, come off it," he snapped. "We heard enough of that nonsense back in town."

"I want to know," Denny rounded on him with a fierceness that surprised them both. "They have to have a reason," he went on, "for pretending it doesn't exist."

Johnson and Armstrong sniggered again.

"We can't ignore the lore of the people when it might give us a clue to what we may find there. Every story is born of truth," he turned to Antonio and said, "is that not so?"

Their guide looked grave and the shadow-play of the firelight seemed to accentuate every feature of his face, sharpening the structure of his bones, making his face seem narrower, more emaciated than it was. The sharpness of the jaw, the deep-set eyes, even the scar that ran up his chest at an angle to the right side of his neck until it reached behind his ear. He leaned in again and spoke quietly, confidingly, but loud enough for the others to hear.

"Listen hard," he said, "it will not be long before we reach the valley rim. Everyone knows this place, they have heard the stories—tales of woodland sprites and faeries, and jungle madness enough to make our children behave for months at a time. As always, there is more to it than this. People do not like to speak of it, do not wish to acknowledge that such a place exists. It fills them with dread, and dread is not a thing a man wants to feel when he is in the jungle, dread born of fear. Fear leads to dread, dread leads to foolishness, and foolishness will lead to death. This is true of all things, do you agree?" Denny nodded, like a schoolboy eager to learn his lesson. "The people fear the valley, but they fear its occupant more. They talk of a beast that lives there—whether one or more, we do not know. It kills without mercy, but is humble. It knows its power and it knows we fear it. It knows that without our guns we are powerless. With every kill it learns more about us. It knows why we never come near its home. How it keeps alive I can only guess. It feasts on flesh; this we know well. We have seen and heard enough to know it. And the sounds we have heard do not bear thinking of. I implore you, listen hard and learn fast, it might prove useful when we get there."

Listen they did, and only Denny appeared to be the one shaken by the story. When it was over, Denny praised the man for his command of a language that was not his own; he spoke it like a gentleman. Antonio blushed.

"Don't encourage him," said Johnson peevishly. "It'll only make him talk more."

Denny said nothing though he wanted to stand and strike his companion. He brushed off the remark and turned again to Antonio.

"What do you think it is, Antonio? A jaguar? Or something else?"

Antonio did not answer, but looked hard at Denny as though he were measuring him for the truth. "I do not know what it is," he said finally. "I have only seen drawings that men have made when they come back. Like my mother said, the men who return come back so changed that it is impossible to think they are the same person. Their skin is the same, but what is inside is not."

"How are they not the same?"

"They are broken, empty." The guide lowered his voice to a whisper as he leaned forward. "It has eaten their souls, I think. All that is left behind is the shell."

"What ineffable *twaddle*," said Armstrong loudly as he got to his feet. "All this talk of eating souls and leaving the shells of men behind? Utter nonsense. You're only trying to scare us, that's what you're doing, isn't it? Got something to hide there, have you?" Then something of a light broke on the poor man. "*That's* what this is all about, isn't it? You're *hiding* something. Something in that valley. Keeping it from the rest of the world so you don't have to share it. You all seem like a poor lot, but I bet you're all *filthy* rich. You just want to act like you're poor so no-one will come look for your treasure troves. Oh yes, you're all very sneaky, aren't you? Got mountains of gold stacked down there, have you? I'll bet that's what it is. Maybe you're even hiding the City of Gold! No matter, no matter. It'll soon be in the hands of the British Empire come the day after tomorrow."

"Yes, quite right," said Johnson, "you'll see. Utter twaddle, yes. Quite nonsensical. The lot of you, greedy swine." Poor Johnson. If only he had a mind of his own to think with that did not include hero worship. With those words they turned to make for their tents and after a while switched their lamp off.

Denny was now alone with their guide. Silence fell on them both. He looked around: the dense thicket would cover the approach of a hunting jaguar, black as night, and they would be none the wiser. They would never see it till the eyes reflected the light of the fire as it watched them, crouching in its hiding place and ready to pounce. Permeating the silence was the cry of cicadas, the chattering monkeys high in the trees, and the yowling of a predatory cat in the distance.

It was not long before the sounds that filled the jungle ceased. Insects refused to take up their call, the jaguar's yowling had been silenced. The jungle was holding its breath.

Denny announced that he would try and get some sleep. "Though I don't know if I will in this deafening silence."

"I will keep watch," said Antonio; "I will keep the fire lit and your companions safe—as best I can," he added with an edge to his voice which made them laugh.

"Thank you," said Denny, and he went into his tent.

While he was getting ready for bed, checking that nothing had slipped into the sleeping sack that had no business being there, Denny watched Antonio through the slit of the tent. He was staring into the fire then looking up into the sky. Then he got up and walked into the thickets. He must have felt the need to relieve himself.

Denny lay down and closed his eyes, trying to find the sleep he craved.

He woke with a start to the cry of an animal nearby. The others had not heard it, for their light was still off, and Denny could hear the loud snore of Armstrong from within. The sound was familiar but he could not find the name for it. There it was again, a low moan with the tinge of a snarl coming from the trees.

It was then that he noticed that Antonio was not where he ought to be.

Denny pulled on his boots, snatched a lamp and tramped off into the trees, eager to see what it was. The cry came again, louder, closer, and notably different from any sound he had ever heard, yet familiar.

There seemed a distinctly human note to the cries he followed. He wondered if his friend was all right, if he was hurt in any way, or if he had fallen prey to the animal that was now calling through the trees. A little way further and the sounds were now the closest they had been. Denny cut the light from the lamp, for the moon now shone full on where the animal was standing. But it was no animal: it was a man. Denny could see Antonio through the thickets, his trousers round his knees, one hand on the trunk of a nearby tree, the other pleasuring his rigid virility. As he stroked, he moaned and gasped and hitched his breath; there was a grunt or two and a cry of ecstasy that Denny did not think it possible for anyone to utter.

As he watched, a memory came and he was pulled back to his days in the all-boys school. There were older boys who did this when in the showers; he had seen them, too, when he, one time when he felt adventurous, snuck out of his dormitory to spy on them. He wanted to know what they did in their free time. There were some that did more than stroke themselves: they stroked one another. Some even went as far as kissing each other and engaging in something Denny did not recognize, not until he was older. It looked painful, but the boys were delighted.

A moment later, a cry of primal delight broke his reverie, and Antonio began to spurt abundantly onto the trunk of the tree. Denny had heard of such a thing being done as a kind of ritual to ensure the protection of the traveller and the prosperity of the tree which would very soon spread its own seed.

Antonio sorted himself and licked his hand, then he said, "I know you are there."

Denny froze.

"You need not feel embarrassed. This is how we protect ourselves in the jungle."

As the guide approached Denny had his head down. He did not want to look at him, for he would see the rash of scarlet that now spread over his cheeks.

"By the looks of it," Antonio added insolently, "you need all the protection you can get."

Denny looked up and the guide smiled at him. It was not an insolent smile, like his words had been, but a genuine one that showed his strong white teeth. He came close and planted a kiss on Denny's lips. The boy flushed worse than before and Antonio went past, heading back to camp.

Was there any need in that? he wondered. Did he really need to go that far?

As he stood there alone, he looked at the tree that Antonio had ejaculated on and, for a moment, wondered if he ought to give it a try himself. His anxieties worked on him, and the kiss sent a surge through his body. His own member now stood to painful attention. He took a step forward and unfastened his britches.

The sensations of his stroking hand came in waves. He grunted and moaned softly as he had heard Antonio do, and his knees started to buckle; he was soon finished. He spurted almost as much as Antonio had and spattered the moss-covered trunk with his pearly essence. Blowing out and fastening himself, he felt shame well within as he walked back to camp.

When they started out the next day the stories of snakes and spiders and fantastic-looking birds and the tiniest but most colourful frogs covered in neurotoxins that would down a man in a minute, came flooding back.

Armstrong and Johnson revelled in the joy of being on the go once more, but their quiet tag-along said nothing and could not find it in himself to share their enthusiasm.

Denny had suffered a sleepless night; the sounds of the forests were mingled, mated with the sounds of human ecstasy, the sounds of fornication.

He would not meet Antonio's eye that day, but he knew the guide smiled to himself in a wicked way.

They hacked through the brush and crossed many hip-deep streams along the way.

It was on such a crossing that a frightening incident occurred. They were assailed by a group of red-and-white banded snakes, so venomous that should they have the chance to bite a fellow, he would be dead in half an hour. In such a place as they were, there would be no chance of getting him the antidote in time, if antidote there was for such beasts. Armstrong and Johnson, they passed without comment; Antonio they ignored completely. It was Denny they seemed to take an interest in. They sped to him, circling him, slithering in and out between his legs and nudging him with their noses, brushing against him with their bodies. On more than one occasion, one of them lifted its head out of the water and opened its mouth, exposing the pink, fleshy inside, the long narrow fangs.

The attack did not last long. The snakes lost interest and left poor Denny standing there, weeping like a child.

It took some time for the others to buck up his spirits. "It is certainly one for the books," they said. They tried to make him see the funny side of things, and they proceeded to ask whether or not he had any blood in him that could charm snakes without having to pull an oboe from his pack. This cheered him up a little, and looking up he beheld the face of Antonio, who looked grave. He stayed silent but regarded Denny with respect it seemed. He did not laugh or join in the jovial attempts to make Denny feel better. They looked at each other for a long time until Antonio dropped his eyes. Once again, he was looking for a sign to see how close they were. He then pointed a long dramatic finger and cried out: "Look! look! There it is! There is the rim of the valley!"

Armstrong climbed up to where Antonio stood and took from his pack a pair of binoculars. It was up a high hill covered by trees. After a little surveying, the explorer made a calculation.

"No more than a couple hours' walk," he said.

"Would it be—what is the word?—*prudent* for us to rest a little longer before we start out?"

Armstrong scoffed. "We don't have the luxury. We keep going. Denny is all better now, aren't you?" he said, clapping Denny between the shoulder blades so hard he was winded.

He nodded but did not speak. He felt a coughing fit coming on.

"Very well," said Antonio, "onwards we shall go."

They went hacking through the trees uphill, coming to the lip of the valley and with joy in their hearts, they looked on their new-found treasure, like kings over their kingdoms.

There are places in the world that defy description; some can describe anything and everything on a whim. But this valley takes time, it needs care. There are multitudes of words that crowd one's mind when they see a place, whether in person or in a photograph: "dazzling", "eerie", "remarkable", "evil". The bowl of the valley was hidden by a thick mist that seeped between the trunks of the trees; one could see the ghostly tendrils reach up into the canopy, through the leaves. Only the tallest trees could pierce this veil of milky white.

What could be seen was strange, almost crooked. They were things that did not seem to belong to this planet. You mustn't think I write of things that come from other worlds, as Mr. Wells has done before me; the idea is more complex than that. Our environment is one that is constantly changing, and has done for the last several hundred million years, since life first walked on it. And over those millions of years there have been changes to the vegetation. Some trees there are that remain and have survived for as long as one can remember, have perhaps seen the changes over those years, have witnessed the birth and death of history, have felt long dead animals climb their trunks and nestle in their branches once upon a time, from the first scattered arthropods to the gigantic dinosaurs that enjoyed such places. And that is what it was to see the valley in person, to feel that one was a witness to millions of years of history caught in a bubble. They stood with their hearts swelling, the air they breathed was the air of success, and they felt the coming tide of fame lap at their feet already.

Antonio broke their reverie. "*This* is the Devil's Pit. This is the home of *raptor*."

They turned as one to face him and stared. Denny spoke first. "Do you mean to say that this monster everyone is so frightened of is an eagle? You have been scaremongering us about some bloody *bird*?"

Antonio, surprised by his words, clenched his jaw. "It is a sacred creature. Sacred and profane. We must respect it. No man in his right mind dares go in. You have heard what happens to the people who do. *Raptor* chooses whether you have the grace to live, or the need to die."

Johnson, for the first time, spoke for himself. "Only God has that power. No other creature has that privilege."

"Well said," said Armstrong, and Johnson could not help but flush and feel tears well in his eyes when he heard his master confer on him a word of support.

"If you wish to enter," said Antonio, "then you will do so alone. I cannot join you."

Denny rounded on him now. "You said you would come with us the whole way."

"I said I made no promises whether or not I would join you entering the valley. I am not stupid enough to risk my hide going somewhere I may never return from. Be warned: this may be the last time you see daylight."

After a little silence and apprehension, Denny was the one to take the first step. He extended his leg in a dramatic manner and stepped on the slope leading into the valley. His eyes met Antonio's, and the guide looked almost forlornly at him. He then smiled and said, "I wish you luck, professors. I truly do."

He turned and ran down the slope and into the jungle from which they came.

Johnson and Armstrong went after him, the latter loading the gun and taking aim. He could not get a clear shot so he let him go.

"The filth," he said. "He won't see a penny from us, that's for certain. He'll get a good thrashing when we get back."

"Oh, he will," said Johnson, "indeed he will."

Denny was not so pessimistic; he thought Antonio would appear soon enough, realizing the error he had made. It wasn't gentlemanly, and Antonio must have known that. Or was it a ruse? The others did not care. They had washed their hands of the whole business.

They reached the belt of trees that took them deeper into the valley, passing into the milky mist, and it stank.

It smelled of rottenness. The rain fell hard on their backs and stung with heat.

They came across a small fresh-water stream and decided to fill their water bags. The plan was to go a little deeper into the valley before nightfall and set camp in the nearest glade, and there cook a meal to celebrate their find.

It was while they filled their water bags that Denny felt something was wrong.

There was a queer sensation, a feeling of being watched by something, and he heard close by a low hiss, like a snake. He lifted his head and looked around.

There was nothing.

Then there was a purring growl and Denny sprang to his feet calling out to the others: "There's something there!"

Now the others were on the alert and both had their guns ready. "Did you see anything there?" said Armstrong.

"No, but there's something here. I heard it. It hissed then growled. It is very close, that's all I can say."

"What did it sound like?"

"Like a snake," said Denny, "but snakes can't growl. It sounded much larger, too."

They did not talk more on the matter, but the discomfort lingered. As they walked deeper into the forest, the feeling of being watched persisted, though they did not mention it, and attached was the feeling that something followed close behind. They could not see it, but it was quite aware of them. The guns Armstrong and Johnson carried gave him some measure of comfort, for Antonio's words came back and echoed in his mind: "It knows that without our guns we are powerless."

We are not powerless, Denny thought. *We have all we need with us.*

Nightfall. The sky was pricked over with stars once more, but this time like they had come to greet the explorers to celebrate their find. They had conquered the superstitions of the natives and entered the heart of their land. There was no need for fear. They poured whiskey for one another and made a great deal of noise. They sang songs drunkenly and made such a racket the beasts of the valley made their own song and calamitous noise. Monkeys howled above them; some threw bits of fruit down in fits of naughtiness. The explorers brushed it off and laughed.

They would return to England heroes; they had conquered a feared and hallowed place for the British Empire, and Armstrong once again talked about how they would be hailed and written of in *The Boy's Own Paper*, his favourite childhood magazine. He talked about how they would be written about in books; perhaps there would be novels too, taking the supernatural things they had heard and making it up like that H. Rider Haggard fellow, or perhaps like Edgar Rice Burroughs in his Tarzan novels.

Johnson was pouring himself another cup of whiskey and Armstrong sat cradling his rifle, resting the butt on the ground. He'd had it with him all day, as if he expected to use it.

Then they heard it, a low, hateful hiss from somewhere in the thickets.

They jumped to their feet, looking this way and that. The sound grew louder, closer. There it was: a purring growl that filled their hearts with horror. And another hiss, a huffing, purring breath from the other end of the glade.

There must be more than one, thought Denny.

Johnson gave a cry. He had seen something in the thickets. He fell back, trying to get away, but his legs crossed and he fell on the fire. His stomach was scorched. Yelling in pain, he rolled off and tried to douse himself and the wound with the water in is bag. His screams seemed to heighten the pleasure of their foes, for now they screamed, taunting them. They then gave a strange barking call from one end of the glade to the other, taken up by the rest of the pack. *Kark! Kark! Kark!* they went, all around, on and on till Denny thought his skull would split. He jammed his fists to his ears to try and block the sounds out.

Something large raced through the glade between them all. Denny thought he'd seen it before it vanished. Bipedal, body kept low to the ground and uncommonly straight when it ran. A slender neck and a long tail for balance. He caught the curious scent of feathers, damp plumage mixed with the dread stench of reptile, so strong it made his eyes water.

The barking calls came again from every direction, then a screech—a high, piercing scream from another world. The trees took up the call in their joyous ecstasy, shrill and clear, a cry from killers who, unlike any animal they had ever seen, played with their prey.

Armstrong gave a cry of surprise as something whipped at his ankle and felled him. For a second or two he was still, looking at his companions before he was dragged screaming into the thickets, arms out, fingers clawing the ground. He was gone.

Johnson gave a pathetic wail, falling to the ground and hugging his knees as he rocked on his rear, his thumb in his mouth like a scared child. Armstrong could be heard from somewhere nearby, still screaming.

A moment or two of those wretched cries, then silence fell.

No monkey howled. No jaguar gave its night-time snarl. The jungle was still as death.

Denny tried to get Johnson to move. They had to get to the lip of the valley and leave. But Johnson would not listen, he would not move.

Then the afflicted man screamed and pointed to the other end of the glade where, beyond the firelight, a shape could be made of the thing that tormented them. Denny and the creature looked each other in the eye.

It was tall—a man's height, he'd said when questioned about it—and held its head high on a long, curving neck. Its eyes were large and green, but the glare of the firelight threw back orange. Denny had, in his youth, seen a medieval Doom painting with demons and devils. The eyes that confronted him now were the eyes of a particular version of the Devil that haunted his sleep for months after. The rest of the face was scaly, all hard and lumpy, but its body was covered with fuzzy plumage; the arms, dexterous and long, held close against its chest, but he saw that the ends of the fingers curved into claws. It made no movement, made no sound, but stood there observing them as if it was learning about them, taking in each feature as Denny did. It was curious about them, especially of Denny.

He made no sound, did not scream like the others had. And the creature stared at him, which was odd for such a thing. Most animals avoided such contact, even among their own. Man and beast stared for some time, then the creature gave a hiss. It lowered its head, its hips raised like a cat getting ready to pounce.

The jungle was holding its breath.

Johnson screamed and jumped to his feet. He made for his rifle, but the creature was too fast. It leaped into the air and struck Denny on the chest, flashing before his eyes on both its feet were two large sickle shaped claws. It jumped again when Denny hit the ground and struck Johnson. He fell on his face, writhing on the ground, whimpering, "Leave me alone! Take him! Take him! Just leave me alone!"

The animal snarled and lowered its slavering jaw, the scaly lips peeled back to show its pointed teeth. It screamed in his face, took his head in its jaws, and sped off into the trees, dragging Johnson with it. Denny could only make out the distinct sound of sobbing as his last companion was taken.

And then there was one.

Denny was alone. The screeching of the animals and Johnson's wails filled the jungle. He turned and ran from that place and made his way to the lip of the valley.

He followed the stream towards the rim and all the while he heard Johnson's distant, terrified screams ring in his ears till they ceased. He heard the beasts of the valley clamour with the ecstasy of a fresh kill, a profane celebration, a mockery of the kind the three enjoyed.

As he ran, he was aware of hissing from behind, of huffing breaths.

Another terrible shriek, that wail from the past went through him. He reached the valley lip, falling to the ground. As he did, he saw one of the attackers run and jump into the air, arms out, fingers splayed, with jaws open and slavering. The claws on its feet would dig into his heart.

With a cry Denny rolled to the side and the creature narrowly missed and tumbled into the thicket behind him.

There was a rustle of leaves and the snarl Denny knew heralded the coming of the beast, but to this astonishment, there came the voice of a man, harsh and full of authority.

"Hey! hey!" it cried. "Away with you! Back to where you belong!"

The animal gave a cry and then fell silent.

Denny waited for the voice's owner to emerge from the bushes. Whoever it was bore a torch. His voice, when it softened, was familiar and welcome. "Professor?" it said.

Denny burst into tears. He threw his arms around Antonio's neck and buried his head in his chest.

Antonio was not alone. A group of villagers had come and made camp, ready to wait for the explorers to come out of the valley. They would take them home when they did. There was a doctor, too. Denny was ill and had to be nursed. The shock, they said; and the doctor talked about *febre cerebral.* Brain fever.

As they listened to Denny ramble about monsters and feathered reptiles, Antonio said, "I feared it was so."

Denny grabbed the doctor's wrist before he left. "Why didn't they kill me?" he said.

"They nearly did," said the doctor harshly. "It is only by luck you are alive right now."

He passed many fitful nights in the villager's camp, dreaming of the Devil's Pit.

No matter how hard he tried he could not shut out the sounds of those creatures.

He could see them, in his dreams, monstrous beasts with dripping jaws, all huddling round his bed, mouths open, ready to pounce.

The bloodied saliva dripped onto his face; he felt and tasted the reek of death on their breath. Round the tooth of one was a signet ring, the ring that belonged to Armstrong. That sound, the purring breath felt so close, so real.

He woke with a start and sat up in his bed, fumbling for his matches. He struck one.

There it was, peering in at him from the tent flaps: a face of scales with larges eyes, and lips curled to reveal many cruel teeth.

It leaped forward and pinned Denny with its foot. The great claw dangled precariously over his heart, the tip teasing his skin like lover's caressing finger. Then pain such as he'd never experienced sliced through his chest as the claw came down and slit his skin.

The beast purred as it lowered its head, baring its teeth once more. Its tongue slid out and licked along his cheek before its eyes met his. The claw drew down his chest. He could feel the blood well to the surface and trickle over his skin, soaking his shirt. But he could not scream. Staring into its eyes, there was a moment or two of hypnosis in which he blacked out, or so he later said. It lifted its foot, turned and sped out of the tent, into the night, its screams echoing through the jungle, rousing the camp.

Denny lay dumbfounded.

He felt as if he had woken from a dream where his eyes had not shut. He sat up once more and struck a match. His shirt drenched with crimson.

There was a long wound that ran from heart to navel, oozing blood.

He found his voice and started to scream. Antonio was there almost instantly, the doctor shortly after. When they saw the wound the doctor barked orders for everyone to keep watch. The beasts of the valley had followed him and might come back.

There was much panic among the people, but the doctor's orders were not ones to be disobeyed.

The wound was sewn as best as could be done; then a poultice was added to prevent an infection. When that was applied, a bandage was wrapped round his torso. Denny cried out: "What was that thing?"

Antonio was silent. When their eyes met, he said only one word.

"*Raptor.*"

There was much ado about getting the only survivor of the expedition home.

Not only had brain fever ravaged the boy but someone, or something, saw fit to wound him before he left. He was removed from the jungle and taken to the nearest city hospital. There he was taken good care of and the priest came daily to speak with him. At times it taxed the holy man's patience, for there was a lot of talk about demons and devils, of beasts that could have survived God's wrath for millions of years.

"The world is a strange place my son," said the holy man. "But there is no possibility of the Devil's work being done here, I assure you. His work is done by those who allow those thoughts into their heads. So, I suggest you don't think any more of it."

Denny said he would try, and the priest agreed that that was all he could ask of him.

It was not long till the chief of police came to visit and started his enquiries.

The interview proved fruitless, but he was confident there was no harm in the boy.

"No," said the priest, when the two met to talk. "Not a scrap of badness in him as I could find, save his obsession with demons and devils."

"Obsession," said the chief of police, now much interested. "In what way is he obsessed?"

"Only that he feels that they trail him, the demons, I mean, and he says he will fall into their hands very soon. He said that they *live* in the Devil's Pit."

"The Devil's Pit?" said the policeman. "A bad place. A very bad place."

"As I have heard."

An uneasy silence passed between them and they crossed themselves, preferring that such a matter be left alone. But the holy man said something which bears repetition.

"He *did* say something *odd*, but I attribute it to the ravings of the fever."

"And what was that?"

"Well, he described the animal that killed his companions, and said…Well…"

The Brazilian chief of police waited patiently for his friend to go on.

"He describes it accurately, though it is impossible to say how it could be. He called it a *dinosaur…*" He went on

104

hurriedly, "N-not that I believe him, you understand. Indeed, it's rather embarrassing to repeat, but I thought it might interest you."

"The world is full of strange things, and full of possibilities. Some of which we, as brilliant as we think ourselves, cannot comprehend," he said. The pair crossed themselves again. They spoke no more that day.

Denny returned home two weeks after the deaths of his friends.

When he docked, he requested meetings with the families of his companions, and told them everything he had seen, sparing the details, but emphasizing their bravery. "They were conscious of the risks," Denny said, "as any explorer should be. And I was only too proud to be with them."

"Could nothing be done to save them?" their mothers asked, though not unkindly.

"I am afraid not…" He did not talk about his escape, though they pressed him and badgered him for an answer. "I cannot say how I got out, for I don't know it myself. I was found and taken to a nearby camp. That is all I can tell you."

"And this fellow Antonio," said Mr. Armstrong. "Do you think he had anything to do with it?"

Denny shook his head. "No, he is innocent. They fell victim to something more powerful than they." He thought of adding, "I wished I was strong enough to save them," but didn't. It would only invite more speculation and more questions.

Later, at the request of *The Boy's Own Paper*, he penned an account of their journey through the jungle.

Boys around the country were reading about the thrilling things seen there, and how only one of three managed to survive. "It is not a story to be told for boys," the account said, "and the reality of it was more terrifying than anyone could possibly imagine."

It was enough to pay off some debts and compensate the families for their losses. It was later sent to a sensationalist paper in France.

"Bad form," many said after they read the account in the magazine to their boys. "Making money from the deaths of decent chaps. It isn't dignified. It's ungentlemanly. Not the way things are done."

Whenever he was met with such words, Denny replied: "It is what they always wanted. I don't think they much cared about how they were written, or what they were said to do, as long as they got on the pages of the *Boy's Own*. I am fulfilling a last and earnest wish. It would be *ungentlemanly* to refuse them *that*."

What follows is an extract from Mr Alastair Denny's journal at the time of his final illness.

I had a visitor last night and I don't know how to conceivably explain the joy I felt when I saw him. Our guide from the T- expedition, Antonio, came to pay a visit. He brought his mother with him, and she was delighted to see me, as I was to see her. They had been very kind to me when I was ill, and I welcomed them heartily.

He looked very much the man of the hour, dressed in his best, looking the part of an English Gentleman. His mother, too, had taken the role of respectable lady, though she looked less comfortable than her son. It must have been very new to her.

I understand how she feels. It took a long time to adjust to life back here after having spent so much time in the wild.

They stayed for some days. We went to London for a while and I showed them all there was to see here. I let them breathe the air of England, and how they relished it.

Back at the house, they seemed to enjoy themselves; Antonio and I spent many hours alone, reacquainting ourselves with one another. When we were done, we talked of our adventure in the jungle. It was impossible to leave the subject unspoken. I told him what I told the priest. I said that what I saw was a dinosaur.

My man shrugged. "Perhaps it was," he said.

"But it's impossible," I said. "A dinosaur, here in the modern world? They've been extinct for sixty-five million years. How can it have survived?"

"Assuredly," said Antonio. "They have been dead a very long time. But things survive and evolve, do they not? That is what your Mr. Darwin has taught us, yes? That things evolve and change and adapt to their surroundings. What if something has lived and hid in the mists and nooks and crannies of the world, evolving internally, but never outwardly. Animals of that kind have lived for as long as the dinosaurs, have they not? Snakes, crocodiles, alligators—they all of them have evolved yet remain unchanged. If all that is possible, why should it not be so for raptor?"

I considered a while and nodded.

He was quite right, of course.

There are thousands of different species that have lived on for time immemorial, and they have never changed. Sometimes they have shrunk, or they have simply got stronger. Spiders have been on earth for nearly three hundred million years, and yet their appearance is no different. They are only, thankfully, much smaller than they were then.

"Perhaps there is a stranger answer. Maybe they were touched by Quetzalcoatl himself?

We laughed and spent the night caressing one another. I felt safe in his arms.

When it was time for them to go, I expressed the wish for them to stay longer. "Alas," my dear friend said, "we are needed back home. We have been away too long."

"Thank you for your kindness," his mother said, and she slipped over my head a thong on which an amulet hung. She smiled and said, "For luck and to keep you safe from bad dreams."

I thanked her and kissed her apple-skin wrinkled cheeks. I think she would have blushed if she could.

Lastly, I said goodbye to my friend. We exchanged looks that I am not ashamed to admit, and when they stood in the doorway, we kissed each other's cheeks—as is customary in France, so I have an excuse. When he turned to leave something strange happened. A curious something affected my friend when the light caught his eyes. They threw back the orange glare of the lamp-light and his smile curled. I saw the impressions of very sharp teeth.

I told myself it was a trick of the light and turned to go back inside.

I lay in bed, reading a book. Then it came: that barking call, that wailing screech. My body went numb and the book dropped from my hands onto the floor.

My mother is not here. And for that I am grateful.

The scar on my chest burns as I write. I can hear them coming up the stairs, their clawed feet tapping the wood of the floor as if patiently waiting for me to come out.

God forgive me. Keep me from the evil I have let in to my life.

A Victorian Drama

A Victorian Drama

Women want love to be a novel, men a short story
Daphne du Maurier

When I was a girl, no more than ten, I saw a woman stand on the gallows, waiting to be hanged. She was bound at the wrists by iron cuffs, and her dress was filthy, stained with mud and, I think, her own excrement. Her face was as dirty and stained as her dress. Her hair was tied tight in a bun, though a few stray locks billowed across her face in the breeze.

She didn't look afraid, or so I thought. She was confident she would meet her maker and He would judge her in his own inviolate, peaceful way.

Not till I was older did I discover what she had done.

And what had she done? Why, she had struck her husband with a rolling pin across his face. When he was down, defenceless—according to the prosecuting counsel—she brought the blows repeatedly till the skull cracked beneath them. The unhappy woman claimed self-defence.

Her husband returned home from work, so the story went, drunk and in a fit of desire. He wanted to have her, as are husbands' wont when with their wives. But, as is often the case after a long day of labour, he found her in ill mood and she scolded him for one reason or other. His desire curdled into rage. He hit her with his fist and grabbed one arm, flinging her violently against a wall. Then his hands were round her throat, choking the life from her.

111

During the struggle, her outstretched hand happened on something hard. With a swing, she brought it crashing against his temple. He let go of her, nursing his wounded face, cursing her. She struck him again, on and on till the skull gave under the rain of blows, when there was nothing left of his features but a bloody, spiky mess of blood and bone and grey matter.

She fell to the floor sobbing when she realized what she had done.

The police came to the door, asking about a disturbance. They were down the street and a neighbour went out in search of a constable, fearing something terrible had happened. The neighbour said she could hear them from her own house across the street. The unhappy woman opened the door to show the horror of her appearance, the face stained with tears, the blood on her skirts and cuffs. That was when the police forced entry and the body was discovered.

She was taken away, by all accounts, as she looked then: spattered with blood and ill.

He husband's body was removed, examined by the inspectors. The woman confessed. I think she always intended to. The investigating inspector had sympathy for her, but murder was still murder, he said, and he was confident that her defence would not hold up in court. Their feeling turned out to be correct—the jury were sympathetic, but she had murdered her husband, when he was down and no longer a threat.

But what if he had intended another attack? Would not she have suffered more, or have been killed herself? None of the jury or judges had thought of that.

She was found guilty and sentenced to death.

The date of execution was set, the time fixed, the place agreed.

My father, a kind man, respected in his circle, tried to keep me from such horrors as the justice system, preferring me to remain indoors with my dolls and dolls' houses, my sewing and stay with my mother. But even he, as loving as he was, could not keep the ugliness of the real world away from me. The fantasy had to be broken. That day was the day the fantasy shattered.

We had taken a wrong turn and found ourselves amid the crowd. We tried to double-back and leave by the way we came, but the jostling bodies that pushed like a relentless current proved too strong. One moment I was holding my father's hand and the next I slipped from his grip. I was pushed forward by a living tide of flesh. The skink of the bodies made me wrinkle my nose.

I found myself in front of the dais, where I could see her face strewn with dirty hair.

She looked out on the crowd to see if there was a sympathetic eye for her. There were none, I fear; she probably had not expected any.

She hardly seemed to care where she was then, not until she saw me. She stared at me, our eyes met and held for a few seconds. The executioner came up behind her and made to slip the bag over her head. She was fretful, animated now, which made the crowd start to cheer and boo. "Get her away from here!" she cried out. "Get the child away!" But it was too late. Her face was covered by the bag, and she stood stone still. A moment later there was a terrible noise, a bang and she fell through the trap at her feet. There was a horrible crack when the noose gave a taut tug and the head went limp, leering to one side. A foot twitched beneath her skirt.

There was silence around me for a matter of seconds that felt like minutes.

The crowd then burst into loud cheering, throwing things at the hanging body of the unfortunate woman. At last my father found me, scooped me up in his arms, and took me away from that awful place. For the first time, I heard my father repeatedly swear under his breath.

I did not cry—indeed, I did not do anything, and said nothing for weeks. But there was a pallor about me, wan complexion and empty eyes.

Mama was furious, though not with me. Her anger was directed at Papa.

This went on for some time, and her coldness prevented her from occupying the same room as he at any time of day. I look back on it and think she made a little drama out of it, as my mother was wont to in times of distress. But the first divide was built, and it would stay there till the day they died.

"She should never have been there," she said fiercely one night, when I was meant to be sleeping. I had snuck out of my room to see what was happening. I wanted my father, for I had had a nightmare, and I heard them talking. Mama took the stage.

"You should have watched her more closely!" I was startled by the vehemence in her voice. She didn't sound like Mama any more.

Papa made no counter to any point she made. They were all correct. We weren't meant to be near that wretched place, even if by mistake. An execution should never be entertainment for the public, where men and women bear their shame and ignominy for the world to see.

The shadow of the woman loomed over me for a long time after.

She often appeared in my dreams, and so disturbed would I be that I would wake in the night and shriek. Always that pale form, her face shrouded by the bag over her head, and when she lifted her hand to grab onto it and pull it off, I would awaken and cry for Papa. He always came when I called. He would soothe me to sleep and sing me lullabies. This went on for some months.

To think of it feels ridiculous, but it has kept some meaning for me, now I am a widow. She had not troubled me for many years; she has come to plague me now. And she is not alone.

No-one has asked me what happened, almost, indeed, like they know the truth, though I know that is not possible. They look at me, observing me, studying me, like a mollusc in the zoological gardens. Their thoughts, their looks, their ideas, have not escaped my notice. And some troublesome creatures with nothing better to do have decided it would be best to try and raise a scandal. I know who is behind it, though I will not commit their name to paper—it is their business and mine. They know, too, I can sue for slander, and that I will win such a case.

I still come to these tea rooms, where the whole thing began, and I am glad of the place and its atmosphere being so very different from the other well-known and respectable cafés. I am free to be myself, free to think, free to not feel like some-one is spying on me or looking at me in some strange way. The common do not care. It exhilarates them and makes them smile that someone of my station might join them in their café, though they do not care for you there. They want to get on with their lives; and this I can do now the trial is over and the murderer hanged.

I can return to normal life and have no worries of the past resurfacing. I write this down for the purpose of exorcism, so that unfortunate creature I witnessed hang long ago can haunt me no longer, that her companion may have a gentle revenge on me. I sit by candlelight to tell the story, and as lawyers demand, it is the truth, the whole truth, and nothing but the truth, so help me God.

It was the day of the ball at the Johnsons', and I had arranged to meet my friend Agatha for a cup of tea, then we would go out into town and find a new dress for her. Agatha and I went to the same school together, and while there we had grown close, finished together, and stayed as we are, the best of friends. As we grew older, and she and I married very different men, she had me as godmother to her children. I would have afforded her the same courtesy, if God had the grace to grant my husband and I a son. I was honoured to be asked and accepted it gladly.

As I made my way to her through the busy streets, carriages hurrying this way and that, the newspaper boys telling the latest headlines, I was aware of the strain of myself going against the current of men, women, and children, of crossing-sweeper boys and chimney cleaners. As I walked I did so unseeing and unseen: indeed, one of the many wonderful things living in a city prescribes; no matter where you are from or who you might be, the city will hide you if you do not wish to be found. Your story means nothing to the man who trod on your dress skirts, the peddler selling roses, the mother holding the hand of her child as they walk the pavements.

In the city you are no-one and everyone.

I reached Agatha's house in plenty time. It was a tall though narrow red-brick affair that sported a bright yellow door, an eccentricity of my dear friend's—the colour yellow being that of the sun—and a symbol of hope for the children when they returned home. I was let in by the maid, Evangeline, and shown into the drawing room where I found Agatha darning a sock. She got up from her task and we kissed one another, she asked for tea and cake to be brought in as we got to chatting.

Agatha was a handsome woman with very fine features, though no-one would ever have considered her beautiful; her high cheekbones, smooth and creamy complexion, and bright eyes all complimented her and her sweetness, though she had been plagued by poor eyesight, given spectacles, they did not detract from her natural handsomeness. After three children she yet had beauty, and to those children there could not have been a more loving mother, and there could not have been a more doting wife for any husband. Always attentive, always considerate, always prepared for the worst, she had a firm grasp on life, a quality of which I was jealous. Her house was run like a naval vessel, nothing wanting, nothing superfluous.

Her husband adored her as much as she did him; a burly man, ruddy-faced, a moustache as thick as a shoe brush and just as black, he was not at all the kind you'd think would have the deepest, fruitiest laughs you had ever heard, nor that he was the loving father he was, doting to all of them, daughters and son. They were the model of the happy family, the kind written about in novels, where there is no trouble, the family the characters strive to be. Physically, the contrast could not have been so strong; but in their personalities, they had found their perfect match.

Today, she sported her lovely burgundy dress with lace cuffs and neck. She looked very much a stately lady. "Darling," she said after we sat down to drink our tea. "This is wonderful, and how very good it is to see you!"

"How are you, Agatha?" I said with beaming smiles.

"Frightful," she said with the air of drama she loved to employ when she had something to discuss. "Absolutely frightful. That dress I had decided on for the Johnsons' ball tonight, you know that lovely rose-coloured one I had spent a fortune on?—ruined, absolutely ruined!"

My jaw dropped. I remembered the dress and made quite clear my admiration for it. To hear that it had been destroyed was indeed a shock.

"What happened?"

"I had asked one of the girls to wash it and make it ready last night, and they had done, but it came back in tatters. The girl who was meant to look after it has no clue how it happened. She was very distressed, I must say."

"A mistake, I am sure," I said.

"Oh, no doubt. But I had to let her go. She had been making too many mistakes of late, and she was really too careless. Now, don't look at me like that, and don't worry. I have written her a good reference, and have requested she be trained by the most effective housekeeper at a friend's city house. If anyone can whip the girl into shape, she can. All is not lost for her. You didn't think I would throw the poor creature out in the street with nothing, did you?"

I could not deny, the thought had crossed my mind.

"No," Agatha went on, "she will be a fine maid, but this was not the house for her."

"Your kindness astounds me," I said.

Agatha blushed. We giggled and embraced.

We discussed the plan of action: we would go shopping to one of the better dressmakers in the city, the one from which I usually acquired my day and nightwear. It would be fruitful, and since she conceded that though she was better at choosing daywear, I was the best judge for what to wear for evening occasions. I too needed a dress for the ball, so I would look around while she looked for her own.

Oh, how I had forgotten the well-known anxieties of young girls when they have nothing suitable to wear for a party! Though I was older, I had forgotten the stresses that presentation always brought when we were to go to an event. The dress must match, it must compliment the parts of us we wanted the men to admire.

Agatha, with her slender frame and handsome features would suit a bright colour, but I was more in favour of the darker shades, for they matched well with my eyes—as so many had told me when I was young.

We ran our hands over the gowns and sought out the colours. The assistant who worked with us had many suggestions. The silhouettes were lovely, but the colours were not right. After a while I became frustrated and went out to find something more suitable for her when I took my eyes from my path and ploughed into the hard chest of a tall man who had been walking in front of me. I blushed and looked up: darkly handsome, auburn hair that flowed over his broad shoulders, and the darkest, most penetrating eyes I had never seen in any man.

I could smell his cologne, filling my mind with the most sensual images. The solidity of him astonished me: a powerful man, a strong man, unlike any I had ever seen before. There was about him, too, that air of power, of authority. He must have been a soldier, on leave from his regiment. My cheeks flushed red. "My apologies," I said, "I wasn't looking where I was going. I should have paid attention."

His voice was low and sensuous, with the American twang of the South. A Texan. I had only read of them in western novels of adventure, the stories of cowboys and Indians. I am not ashamed to admit, even as a married woman, that he inspired in me a strange feeling, one which I had not felt since the early days of being admired, the first days of my marriage. Like a girl of sixteen once again, I couldn't help but stare, then I caught myself and turned away, apologizing again. I dismissed myself and wandered among the dresses.

As I went and picked out a few more gowns, I heard the American talking away in another part of the shop. I looked up and saw he was looking at me still from the other side. His presence unnerved me, unsettled me; no man had had that power since the first days of my husband's courtship. And he was a handsome man in those days, though they are now a time I have very little connection to. It might have been the feelings inspired that had driven me away from him, that made my cheeks burn with that forgotten but tumultuous desire. I lowered my eyes to the dresses and picked out more, then returned to Agatha.

"Is everything all right?" she asked. "You seem a little distressed."

I waved away her concern and told her I was more than all right, then I watched as the assistant stripped Agatha of the last gown tried on and slipped her into the next. At last we got to a dress she liked and one I liked too. It was a mixture of silk and chiffon, like her last, and it was a deep pink that suited her complexion perfectly. It was my turn next, and I went onto the shop floor once more to find something.

There was a gorgeous satin thing I had had my eye on since we were browsing; midnight blue with rhinestones in its skirts, so that it sparkled like the night sky. I asked the assistant if it was available to be tried on and she said it was; I was taken to the fitting room and immediately I fell in love with it. It was a good fit, and suited me perfectly. "Does *madame* like the fit?" the assistant asked, a French girl with a flair for making her customers feel like she was in Paris on a day of summer, getting ready for a masquerade.

"Yes," I said, "I like it very much. I will take it."

"*Mais oui, madame,*" the girl said and flashed me a smile with brilliantly white teeth.

The dress was taken off, packed away and paid for when we turned and the American, standing against the pillar outside the great shop, stepped toward us and said, "My apologies, for my rudeness earlier I mean, I should have said something."

My cheek burned again, and I did my best to hide it. I could tell that Agatha was the same. We had both turned into girls of sixteen, at a ball somewhere, and the handsome stranger had come to pay his respects and perhaps ask one of us to dance. "There is nothing to apologize for, I can assure you," I said. "It was she who was not looking where she was going, and I collided with you."

"And I said nothing to soothe your anxieties," he countered, "and for that I must surely say something."

"You are very kind, sir," I said, smiling as best I could, but wanting to get away quickly. I had no time to be there, but something made me stay.

"Allow me to introduce myself," he said, "Damien Erisa, formerly of Texas." He put out his hand. I placed mine in his and he kissed it softly. He did the same for Agatha. "May I invite you to a cup of tea, to acquaint ourselves?"

"That would be very well, Mr Erisa," I said, "but we really—"

"Of course, we would love to," Agatha cut in. I was surprised. She had never been this eager to indulge a stranger when they had just met. As we walked, and Mr Erisa led us to a part of town I was not familiar with, she whispered in my ear, trying to sooth my protestations. "We have never met a live American before. It will be an education. And indeed, I wish to question him to see if he is truly from the land of the free." She hurried on to walk by his side as I trailed behind. Something of horror rose in me, not knowing what she was going to do or say. She had a propensity for saying the wrong thing, though it was never meant maliciously.

Inside Aunt Adelaide's Tea Rooms, we were seated in a part of the shop where we could not be disturbed, and the waiters brought us tea, plates of sandwiches, and an angel cake. These were the well-known feasts of Aunt Adelaide's, who specialized in baking of this kind. She had received high praise from all over, it appeared, even had been reviewed in a local newspaper, no doubt allowing her to capitalize on her fame. But the people came, and her cakes were baked to perfection. People paid good prices for them, and they were never let down.

What a cake we had before us! I took a bite into my slice when it was given and it melted in the mouth almost instantly in an explosion of sweet flavour. My own cook could not have made anything finer, and she was just as skilled!

The topic of talk turned to Mr Erisa after we had sampled the cake and drank our tea. A simple sojourner, he called himself, coming to visit his family on these shores, just in time, it seemed, for the Civil War was raging in his country, and men fell on both sides, and the future of thousands hanging in the balance. Agatha, ever a warrior for justice, started asking him what were his views on slavery, and I am ashamed to say I resented her for it. It did not, it appeared, seem to bother our guest.

"I am a simple believer," he said, "that no man ought to be clamped in chains."

"Yet you allow it to happen, and have done since the beginning of your country." Once she started, there was no stopping her. I tried to turn the topic of conversation, but Agatha did not pay it any heed. "It is quite remarkable," she went on, "that someone can think another man deserves to be in chains—oh, yes I know you say you don't believe they should—but that must mean you think that a slave is a man and not an animal, as many Americans I have met have told me."

An uneasy silence followed; again, I tried to stop her, but she was not listening.

"We women are treated very much thus," she said, "though there are no chains on our wrists, as you see, or on our ankles. We are bound by something else. Only by the dictates of a masculine race are we kept, a race that knows nothing about us or what we suffer. They say we are lesser than they, you see. Always have. That to be a man is to be superior. But leave a man in a house alone with no-one to help him, everything will be turned upside down. With no-one to help manage house for him, his kingdom crumbles, do you not agree?"

She looked to me for support, but I said nothing. Whether or not she resented my new-found silence, I don't know, but she continued.

"It is we women who must do it all. Bear the children, raise them, feed them, make sure the house won't fall around our ears. Are we not the sex that has an eye for detail, who plan the parties that allow husbands to be seen as respectable and gracious? We women put in most of that work; the husband has very little to do with it. We cook, we bake, we sew, we can make it all from scratch, we do charity work, we organize important events much better than any man ever could. Yet we suffer from our men folk when they are dissatisfied with the ordering of the world."

She was becoming unbearable now, and I felt something hot and heavy rise in me, from deep within, a blazing flare of temper I feared would bubble to the surface and burst as soon as it reached us.

"But we," she went on, "we women bear it all. Silently, lovingly, because we must. But we ask only to be loved, to not be saddled with brutes who would take advantage of us."

As she talked, I noticed that there was a swift glance to me. I felt his eyes burn my skin and penetrate my heart. I tried my best to ignore the thudding in my breast, this silly school-girl desire coming over me, but I could not. Now Agatha had stopped talking, and I said not without harshness, "I quite agree, Agatha. But I do not think Mr Erisa will take too kindly to us tarring men with the same brush as they do us women. It is not dignified of us. If we are to be seen as something other than what they think, we should not allow our resentments to show."

In an instant she was subdued and silent, and I hated myself the moment I said what I did. I had seen this submissive, *piano* state many times before when we were children and I had been invited, as a special mark of favour, to her parents' house in town. She was a girl who had her mind always in the future, dreaming up impossible things, but at times she would be proved right. Her mother felt it uncanny, and chastised her vehemently. "If you are like this when you meet a young man, you will never be married. Who wants a girl who can think of other things when she should be thinking about her children and husband?"

Yes, I had heard it all: she would end up a lonely old maid, the sport of little louts and children with stones, and any man with an impudent tongue. Though she fell silent every time, she never learned her lessons. She burned with a passion that would never leave her, but to now hear it from a friend who had been by her side and supported her through it all, must have been a shocking blow to her, a betrayal as disgusting as that of the friends of Julius Caesar. I thought to myself: *How could I be so cruel?* The memory of her mother was a bitter one, even when she came to be by her bed as she lay dying, she had always that critical eye and always had the power to remark on something that destroyed her confidence. Anything from her appearance, to the station of her husband and his ability to earn (which was a silly remark really, since he made a very decent amount of money), to the condition of her children, she would pick at it and make sure Agatha knew how she felt. It must have been a mercy to Agatha when she died, and I can't feel sorry for thinking it.

But my harshness shocked me. I put out my hand and took hers. She smiled, that weak, affirming smile, telling me she was all right.

"I merely mean to say, we don't want to scare off our new friend, do we? He might think we are planning to convert him."

Agatha laughed gently and found her gay spirits again.

"Then consider me converted, ladies," said Mr Erisa. "I find it only too true what your dear friend says. Women take the brunt of everything we men have to do, and they get so little credit for it. We say they shouldn't get it. But that's all bullshit."

The power of his profanity astonished us, and the moment he said it his hand went to his mouth like a player on the stage in mock-shock. But his apology was sincere enough. "You will have to forgive my coarse tongue," he said. "Spending as much time among men and with the likes of cowboys is enough to turn anyone into a savage. But I am glad I have you both at my side to teach me proper manners."

We all laughed and went on with our tea.

As we were leaving the shop he asked, "Will you be appearing at the ball tonight?"

"There is a ball at the Johnsons we are attending," I said.

"That's the very ball I'm talking about. The Johnsons are my relatives."

As we bid each other goodbye, we hoped to see him again tonight and hopefully ask for either of our hands when the time came to dance. He kissed our hands, tipped his hat, and went off at a pace in the opposite direction.

I asked for a bath when I returned home and my hair was washed, dried, and styled to suit the new dress I had bought. Daisy, my lady's maid, gasped when it was taken out of its box. I had asked if she could help me get into it, though it was her day off, she had come home early. I did not like asking her when she might have had plans, but she said that it would be no trouble. She loved it as much as I did, and I wondered what she would look like in it. She was young and a sight prettier than I was. I had grown older, and I felt she would look much prettier in it than I ever would.

As I got ready, letting my hair dry and as Daisy laid the dress out, I let my mind wander to times long gone, but still very present. I could not help but think about the days before my marriage and the days during. I looked to the bed where Daisy spread the dress out and smoothed it. My husband and I slept in separate rooms, so there was no chance he would interrupt me in my vulnerable state of nakedness. He would not dare enter this room, wouldn't dare come near me at all these days, for he deigned to ignore me. Only when we had company would he act like he loved me and acknowledged my existence. We were obliged then to act as if we were in a happy union; when company was removed, the stage was very different.

We would not speak, would not touch one another, indeed, would not give each other the satisfaction of a fleeting glance. The reasons I knew well enough, for I imposed them.

He had been sharing his bed with the parlour maid, Mary. I had known there was some kind of liaison going on between my husband and someone else for some time, but I could not have guessed it was lithe, quick-witted, high-spirited Mary with her graceful school-girl features, her tangle of dirty blonde hair, her bright eyes, her laugh which rocked the whole room when she uttered it. Sweet, pretty, conniving Mary. Who would have thought she was capable of such treachery?

I had the misfortune to witness the consummation of their affair one night when I was bed-ridden. Bored out of my mind, and with the servants mostly in bed, I did not wish to rouse them or the rest of the household with pulling the bell rope, so I stole down the stairs and got to the library when I heard the sound of grunting from within. I froze then, putting my ear to the door and listening. More muffled grunting, and the high gasp of a woman. I burst into the room and saw them making love. She was against a bookcase, her arms and legs wrapped round him, and he thrusting into her with savage passion. He was always so loud; it was a wonder he did not wake the rest of the house. With a strangled cry, he climaxed and she whimpered to feel him do so. Then her eyes fell on me. "Stop! stop!" she cried.

"What's the matter?" he said then he turned.

Our eyes met for a few seconds before I turned from the room and left them alone.

I locked myself in my room that night, forcing myself from letting my husband in when he came to explain. He twisted and rattled the knob trying to force the door, calling my name, saying he wanted to tell me everything. I did not let him in. I took breakfast in my room. When I at last allowed him entry, he said: "I am so sorry," but I stopped him. "I don't want to hear anything of it," I said, "and if you have any respect for this house, you won't talk of it, ever. Is that understood?"

With his head hanging, he nodded his assent and left the room like a scolded child.

We remained in separate rooms, even after my illness. I mention it, but fear it is painful enough for me to remember: I lost a child and the stillbirth had gone wrong, and left me on the verge of death. Only by the graces and skill of very talented doctors did I survive. I had to have plenty rest; I should have no shocks lest it send me over the edge once more. I did not go back to my previous condition, but it left only the greatest anger in my heart. We did not talk about it; I did not wish to. And he respected my wishes enough to leave me alone. At dinner we were good enough to show our faces, but we did not speak. I wondered for a long time what the staff thought about us, if they knew but were not brave enough to tell me. In many ways, my patience with them wore thin, and I took out that anger on them. Three dismissal over trivial accidents, another because something was said amiss and I would not tolerate insubordination. I wonder now what they thought of me when I went through that stage of madness, of cruelty I astounded even myself with. Had I the chance to go back and change it all, I would; the shame of that time hangs heavy on me now. But there is no chance now;

what they think of me is how they will no doubt remember me.

I wondered, too, if everyone of our acquaintance knew the truth; that my husband was a philanderer, and adulterer. Did they know he had a mistress installed in our house when I, at the time, was teetering on the door of death? Why did they not tell me? Was it embarrassment they felt for me, or did they prefer I found out for myself? I wondered how long they had been lovers, if I really was so stupid as to not guess it was someone in the house. But I knew he had someone on the side—apparently all married men have a mistress, but I find that statement a hard one to believe. I only know about mistresses in novels, not in reality. Now I was living that fiction, and I did not know how to address it other than with anger and resentment to my own servants.

Dragging my mind back to the present, my hair dried now and the dress ready for me, I stood and allowed Daisy to tie round my waist the hoop-skirt, then cinch my corset as tightly as she could, then slipped into the gown, fastening the stays one at a time. When it was done, I looked in the mirror and observed myself. Daisy had tears in her eyes. "Oh, madam," she said with genuine emotion. "You look so pretty, if you pardon me saying so."

For the first time, I smiled, and said, "Thank you, Daisy. That's very kind of you to say. Do you think I ought to wear any jewels tonight? A choker, perhaps?"

She considered a moment and said, "A choker might be best, madam." She picked out a simple thing for me with a diamond dangling from it.

"Yes," I said at last, "yes, that looks very pretty indeed, and it goes well with the dress."

"Yes, madam."

When I went down the stairs, I knocked on my husband's study door and said, "I will be going out now. The Johnsons will be expecting me."

George was writing at his desk; the scratch of his pen was the only sound in the room, the crackle of the fire barely audible. He didn't look up or see the gown I wore. He did not say, "You look lovely, darling." The time for such niceties had passed, and I allowed them to. I had ensured the coldness between us. He said, "Very well."

"I won't be back late," I went on, "so you needn't stay up for me."

Why was I telling him this? The coldness could never be bridged, yet I still wanted some connection with him. He was, after all, still my husband. He made no reply, the scratch of his pen stopped. An awkward silence filled the room and I felt the shameful start of tears behind my eyes.

"Don't stay up working too late," I said then turned from the room.

At the foot of the stairs I was met by Green, the butler. He was a man with the drooping face of a basset hound, the fluid contours of his cheeks hanging in folds, his lower lip jutted out a little comically, like a caricature, though he was in every degree the opposite. He was a good man, and a loving one. I had known him since I was a girl, since his father was butler to my father—and taking his father's place, I knew I had in him a trusted ally. This did not protect him from my coldness to the other servants when I discovered the amour between my husband and Mary and I was harshest to him out of all the servants; my ally had let me down, and he would suffer for it, I thought.

But here he was, standing at the foot of the stairs, ready to see me out. He was a butler of great skill, who cared for us so much we considered and treated him as family. There was a place for him in any room, and we told him our every worry.

There was always a lesson in what he told us, and often he would prove to be right. Every house needs a butler like Green, I think—though I fear his kind are a dying breed. I smiled at him and he smiled back. He said, "Will you be out late, Mrs Campbell?"

"No," I said, "keep the door unlocked. I will not be late at all."

"Very good, madam," he said.

I stepped out into the night and into the cab that was waiting for me.

For no reason known to me, I felt like Cinderella in her carriage made of a pumpkin on her way to meet the prince at the grand ball. It was a cold night with a little rain, a change from the heat of the day earlier. I was grateful for my choice of wearing a cloak as I clutched it tight around my shoulders and breast.

Outside the world was putting itself to bed. Shops were closed, linen drapers put their shutters up to signify they would do no more business that day; men and women chatted loudly and went about their lives as merrily as could be expected, and I remember how I envied them their ability to talk to their friends, their spouses, even their children. Though I had friends, I could not talk to them about my predicament, the results which I'd received for my coldness; I couldn't talk to them about anything of that kind. It would not be proper, not generous. But it had to be at some point. How much longer could I go on in silence? The thoughts of leaving the house forever crossed my mind, affecting a separation might be the only way we could live apart and not fear any scandal. So many marriages ended thus, but to ask for a divorce was out of the question, as desirable as it might be. To separate myself, body and soul from my husband, was my greatest ambition.

The cab turned into the driveway of the Johnsons' property and stopped outside the door. I envied the house—not a town house, for it had space and a large garden in which the family could rest themselves, relax, and take tea with guests when the days were warm. I wished I had a house of this kind to myself, but George decided a town house would be best, and convenient for his travel to work and back. I hated when the fog rolled in, smelling of the sea, rancid and the soot fell from the great belching chimneys of factories elsewhere.

I stepped from the cab and paid the man's fare, turned and was greeted at the door by Agatha. We kissed each other on the cheeks and smiled. My cloak was taken from me and hung up on a peg by one of the maids. I noticed she was quite unpretty, and I envied that, too. What if Mary had looked like that, blotchy-skinned, piggy-eyed, with rounded cheeks? Would George have taken her anyway? I pushed the thoughts from my mind, trying to soothe the anger in me so I could enjoy myself. I would not have my evening marred by bitterness; I was going to enjoy myself. The house was splendidly large, the kind of house in which a family could be raised in happiness, and there was happiness here, the very atmosphere crackled with it. And the people around us beamed with smiles and chatted with each other quite merrily. The fashions were the latest from all over the continent, the best London could provide, though some of them exposed a little too much shoulder and bosom for my taste (my upbringing could not allow me to let it slide as easily as others did). I felt that to expose myself thus would be like parading around the house like Lady Godiva.

Agatha milled me through the different groups and introduced me to new faces. There were too many ladies and gentlemen for me to remember, and half way through talking, I was astounded to find I had already forgotten their names. I felt shame well within me, but I didn't know why: it was surely normal for many people to forget the names of those met at parties of this kind, and I was suffering from it now. When we were done with the talk, we came at last to Mr and Mrs Johnson, who gave us full smiles and embraces. We had known each other for years, almost as long as Agatha and I— for she was at the same school as we, and she made a perfect match, it appeared, and had the family to prove it. Her children were above, settling down for the night. The first guests had arrived and they were allowed to dance a few dances, eat some food, then were packed off to bed. We would not be seeing them again tonight, she said regretfully. But there was someone she wanted everyone to meet, and he was eager to meet everyone too.

From another side of the room, Mr Erisa had appeared. I heard his loud American voice slice through the mirthful atmosphere and chatter with his own immense bellow of a laugh, a sound I had never heard before or since. We all turned; some of the ladies' cheeks coloured to the sound. I found it at once ridiculous, but somehow endearing.

"We met Mr Erisa earlier today," said Agatha to Mrs Johnson, when the laughter had at last subsided. "He is a veritable gentleman, I must say."

"Indeed, he is," said Mrs Johnson. "We are proud of all he has done. Though it is strange to see him here."

"In what way?" I asked.

"Well, we have never met. His letter came out of the blue, saying we were related on the side of some aunt or other, and that he wanted to meet his British relatives. I was sceptical at first, as anyone would be," she added, as if she thought we judged her, "but he knew much about my aunt, my father's sister who went to the Americas and wed a man there. She had had many children, by all accounts. He gave me a description of her, and recited stories she had told him, stories I knew very well, because I was there to witness them." Her eyes misted over, as they do when one talks of their childhood; that wistful, longing stare into nothing, like the world around her had fallen away and she was there again, as a child, watching whatever her father and aunt were doing. "It was, indeed, quite a surprise to find a relative who has lived so adventurously in the Southern States. Though he was forced to flee when the war started."

"Yes," I said, "we discussed the ideology of it when we met."

A disapproving glance from Mrs Johnson met us. It wasn't good form to talk about the problems of one's home.

"But I hope he is enjoying his stay with you," said Agatha.

We went away and mingled with the other guests. The dancing was about to begin, and I had confined myself to a chair in the corner of the room, quite content to watch the gaiety as it unfolded. I smiled at young lovers, kept back my tears at old ones. Agatha went with her John and I was alone without George. My bitterness welled in me again, and I felt my tears for others turn to tears of fury, the anger of three years' knowing he wanted another woman, had bed her, and while I was ill, he made sure I could never go near him. He had made himself so repulsive to me, almost like he wanted the separation to come true. Though he never asked for one, never suggested one. That was always in my mind. But how could it be otherwise? He loved another woman, and had so run out of love for me.

The quartet, which was staged at the other end of the room, started playing one of our traditional tunes. The dancers danced, milling in and out of one another, taking hands and spinning round and round. My mind started to wander, and I stared at their forms, the dresses ruffling and twirling in a blending kaleidoscope of colour.

I closed my eyes and lost myself to the sounds of the music.

"May I have the honour of the next dance," the familiar voice of Mr Erisa said. I opened my eyes and smiled up at him, as he smiled down at me, offering me his hand.

I nodded and took it gratefully. My cheeks did not colour; I was glad of the attention he gave me, for it made me feel like a wanted woman again. If my husband did not want me, then I would find a man who did. Why must I be the one who should bear it in silence, be the woman who is patient, wait for her husband to somehow learn by some agency of the supernatural or by magic, that all he did was wrong? My patience had worn thin, and I would enjoy my night.

When the tuned rolled off into nothing, the dancers got back to their previous positions and faced their partners. We did the same and I held my gaze, looking right into his eyes. He smiled a strange, wolfish smile, the smile that lets one know they intend to impress. A smile I had not seen on the face of George, but on every other man I had known.

The new tune began and we took hands and started to dance, twirling and spinning. He pressed me close against him for the waltz and we did not take our eyes from one another. He was a skilled dancer, a fact which greatly impressed me.

I did not lose composure to this; I knew I was being watched. A married woman dancing with a much younger man, a *handsome* man at that. Tongues would wag and rumours would fly. Let them, I thought. They knew more about my situation than I did, so let them talk, let them say anything they pleased. There would be no need to confront them, they knew my husband was unfaithful. How could they not? Men brag about their conquests; we women are modest by half, though I have known some who brag as bad as a man.

The tune quickened, and so did we. This way and that, under and to the side, spinning out then back in, my back against his chest when we were done. I turned my head a little awkwardly to look at him, and he looked down at me, his eyes burning deep and dark. My heart hammered in my breast, and I felt myself tremble with desire.

He bowed and I curtsied, then I turned from him and hurried away somewhere quiet so I could gather my thoughts. He had aroused in me the desires I wish I had once again for my husband, the urges of a union which ought to have brought forth children. I felt shame in me again, the same shame that afflicted me when I could not bear a child to term, could not bring our son into the world and allow him to live happily. We would never watch him grow, never watch him achieve all that he might have achieved, and it was my fault.

I was on the verge of tears when I stepped out into the garden where I would be alone. There was a bench at the far end hidden by some trees; on my day visits to the Johnsons' house I sat there many times to collect my thoughts, rest from the day's activities, and keep out of the sun. I was very fond of it as a small hiding place. I wanted to be there now, wanted its safety, its isolation. As I made my way across the lawn and to the trees where the bench stood, I noticed that someone followed; tall, dark, and the light from behind shone like a halo on his fiery hair.

He followed, and I advanced a little quicker into the safety of the trees. After a second, Mr Erisa appeared. I was sitting on the bench and my breath caught in my chest. "You seem a might lonely out here," he said. "I thought you might like some company."

I shifted a little on the bench to allow for him to sit with me, and he did so.

We were silent for a few seconds when he turned to me and said, "You seemed a little distressed after the dance. Was there something wrong?"

I shook my head but did not answer. How could I tell him of the feelings he aroused in me when we danced, how he made me feel wanted and loved, though he was not my husband? I wanted to burst into tears and press my face against his shoulder, and I hated that I felt it. In the space of a short day, I had been made to feel feeble and incapable of being a good wife, cold and cruel; stand-offish and blunt. I did not want to be like that for ever. I wanted to be a loving wife, a wife who would greet her husband with a kiss when he came home, have his meal ready for him, sit with him in the drawing room before the fire and let him talk about the things he had done at work, nod and smile and let him go on. And if he wanted my opinion, I would give it happily. These things I wanted, but for certain I would never have.

Then I did something I never thought I'd dare do. I turned to him, took his face in my hands and kissed him, on the mouth, passionately, urgently. We were locked thus for a moment or two, and I did not feel any resistance from him. When I pulled away and realized what I had done, I apologized, said a few words which I do not now remember, then he took my face in his hands and returned the kiss with the same urgency, the same passion. I felt his hands on me as we were entwined, his tongue questing the space of my mouth, as my own tongue quested his and they met in euphoric dance.

When the kiss broke, I sat there panting. My face burned with desire. Automatically, my hand went to his virility, which was rigid now, as eager to be pleased as I was. Our kisses turned hot and needy, and my hand clutched at his bulging, throbbing manhood. He groaned as I did and his hips moved, thrusting his member against my fingers. At last, I undid his britches and let his virility loose. He was larger than I thought he was, but that did not matter. I stood and straddled him as he sat on the bench, lifting my dress and pulling the front of my drawers down so he could enter with relative ease.

His length impaled me like I were a virgin again with my husband on our wedding night and I felt the sensations, coming in waves hard and fast. I ground my hips over him and gave out little cries of ecstasy when I heard him beneath me, his face pressed against my breast, grunting and uttering soft groans as we made love under the trees. The cold night air did not impede us; the sensations brought the blood pumping through my veins quicker than ever, and my whole body felt like it would catch fire with our lovemaking.

At last, I threw my head back and gave a cry, louder than I wanted, when I reached my crises at last. My body shuddered, and beneath me I felt him throb inside. With a heavy grunt he came, and I could feel the twitch of his member as his seed spurted forth. I gasped and panted as everything came to an end. He stayed inside me for a while longer till his rigidity subsided. When he pulled himself from me and fastened his britches, he looked at me as if he were saying, "We will never speak of this." I nodded my assent; he did not need to say it.

I went back to the house first and went inside. I felt cold suddenly, the sweat from my experience had become chill, and when I found Agatha once more, I sat with teeth chattering as I went into the dining room. Hot food would do me good, and it did.

I did not see Mr Erisa come in at any time. No doubt he had gone to his room to freshen himself.

Or was it because he could not now be seen in the same room as I?

After the meal, I said I was ready to go home and would get my cloak.

"Shall I summon a cab for you?" asked Mr Johnson.

"No, thank you," I replied. "I would much rather walk."

This astounded the people listening. A woman walking home in the dark?

Agatha was beside herself with worry. She tried loudly to get others around us to see her way of thinking, that a woman such as myself, without a chaperone, must take a cab. At last, I became irritated, but I would not allow myself to be as cruel as I was earlier in the day. I said at last, "We must show these men that we are not dependent on them to protect us. Let me show them." I brought my voice to a whisper with the last sentence, conspiratorial, like we were once again children, keeping secrets from our *madame* in school. She reluctantly let me go, and out I went into the night, down the drive, out the gate and into the street, heading for the city. At the city boundary, I would hail a cab and have him drive me home, but for now I wanted to be alone and walk; I wanted to think about what had happened at the party, and soothe the shame welling in my stomach, heavy like a ball of lead.

How could George do it? I asked myself as I walked, the world around me invisible, and I was invisible to the world. How could he do it without feeling this tremendous guilt? It wracked me from head to foot, and I trembled with it, and my chin was never still the whole way. The tears welled and misted my eyes over, and with some anger I brushed them away with the back of my hand. Why should I feel this? Why should I feel this resentment myself now that I was no better than my husband?

And then it struck me: I felt shame because I had done the same as he, and I did it without such a feeling. I threw myself at Mr Erisa's feet and he had gladly accepted me as a lover.

The air about me was cool, thankfully not as cold as it had been when at the Johnsons'. I pulled my cloak around me tight and hurried on. The city boundaries were near, and I made to hail a cab which would take me home. I told the driver the address and got in. Once inside that narrow box, the anxieties of a thousand women crammed themselves in with me. I would have to keep it a secret from my husband; he must never know. He would have grounds for a divorce should he discover it, and I would be disgraced. The evidence would be sufficient for him; for me it was not so. I needed ten counts, and he needed two. The odds were stacked against me, as they say.

As the cab turned corners and shook a little as it went over cobbled roads, I thought of Mary. I would have to be wary of her. She all of a sudden had become a terrible, malicious figure in my life, with the power to protect or destroy me. I had an inkling of what she would choose, were she compelled to do so. The idea of blackmail rose in my mind and was determined to be a nuisance. My heart was a flutter, but not as it was almost two hours hence; the anxiety would not abate, even when I told myself I was being silly. My scattered thinking would not come to heel, like disobedient hounds who are seized with fits of naughtiness.

I arrived outside the house and paid the driver his fare. He was off in an instant as soon as I got out the cab. I stared up at the house and wondered what I ought to do next. Should I pretend everything was normal, that nothing had happened between a stranger and myself? Or would I be brazen and full of life when I made my entrance? I had a second to decide before I turned the handle and went inside. I had chosen the coward's way and was quiet. I pretended I had had a lovely time at the party and that nothing had happened. I hung up my cloak on a peg by the door. I climbed the stairs and headed to my room when the door of my husband's study opened. He was still up; I hadn't noticed the sliver of light under the door.

"Ah, there you are," he said. He looked embarrassed about something. "Could you be so kind as to come in. I wish to have a word with you."

My stomach dropped, turned icy cold.

If I could reverse the clock, take back every word spoken, every action committed, I would do so in a heartbeat. But that is not the way of the world, and we rarely ever get second chances when we say and do things that can never be reclaimed. Even Mr Dickens with his brilliant imagination could not bring back the years to rectify the mistakes of the past, nor *Monsieur* Verne with his fantastical machines and impossible worlds. Our mistakes are what make us fallible, what make us human. They are the chisel blows by which we are made, are they not?

I went into the study like a child who has been summoned to her father's room to answer for some trifling misdemeanour which has been blown out of proportion, but which the father has no intention of letting slide. I had to hide my fear—I could not let him know something happened while I was at the party.

He closed the door behind him, and lingered there a moment. He stared at something I could not see, like he was trying to muster the courage to meet my eyes. He had been doing that a good deal of late, and my scolding tongue had given him no chance to be courageous. I said nothing now; I knew he wanted to speak to me about something important. If I had to have an interview in his study, then quite naturally it would be important.

"A good party?" he asked nonchalantly.

"Yes," I said. "A good party."

"The Johnsons are well?"

"Quite well."

"Good." His thoughts seemed to trail away, which he was doing a great deal more of as the months went by. "Good, I am glad," he said at last. "Get up to anything?"

A stab went through my stomach, hot and cold all at once. My heart thumped against my ribs.

"Not really," I said. "I danced a few dances and observed the people worth observing; a few a little too easy for my taste. Fashionable dresses, wide mouths, broad noses and an exposed bosom or two. Not like when we were young."

He chuckled. I had not heard that sound in three years. He rarely laughed with me, and I missed it so. I grabbed hold of the thread that dangled before me with both hands. "You never failed to make me smile when we poked fun at the other dancers and guests at parties," he said. I felt elated. He remembered something of us. My knees went weak and my chin trembled as he spoke.

After a moment or two the laughter died from his face and he sighed. As quickly as the happiness came, it had vanished of a sudden, and I did not know whether or not it would come back.

"There is a matter of great delicacy which I must discuss with you," he said. "It concerns us both very much, and I would very much like your cooperation."

I felt the anger come back into my body and I felt my fists clench.

"And what is it you wish to discuss," I said.

"It is about Mary…"

Then I exploded. I knew it. He would wish for a separation or a divorce, and I would be left in disgrace. I turned on him and said something, I can't remember what, but I know they were furious words. I saw him shrink back then gather courage to oppose what I said.

"You have always been treated amicably in this house," he said.

"*Amicably*?" I repeated, my voice rising to a shriek. "In what way have I been treated as amicably as you suggest?"

"We have always kept out of your way, knowing it would upset you."

"And that is enough to say I have been treated with amiability? If you wished to do that, you should have packed me away somewhere where I would never have to hear it or think of it happening. But it did and it does. Every night. I can hear it from my room, through the walls. I have never known such cruelty to occur. And if I have, it must surely have been in some novel or other."

"It was a liaison that got out of hand. It should never have happened."

"Indeed; but it did happen, and I was left thinking that it was my fault. I wondered every day if it was because I could not have a child for you, could not bring our son into the world. On the verge of that happening, I have a stillbirth, and in recovery you find the parlour maid to have your way with."

It was all coming out. My anger, my bitterness, my contempt. All had found their way to my voice, and they spilled forth in some unending torrent that would never slow, would never subside. A dam within me had given, and what was held back came spilling out in all its glory. There was nothing he could say to counter what I said; he stood there in stunned silence and listened to everything. The expression he wore made me give pause. I must have not looked like the woman he had married any more, and it frightened him.

But I did not care any more, and I went on without caring.

"Was I only a prize for you, George? Was I only a trophy, a conquest which you could parade to your friends, like a knight come back from slaying the dragon at my gates? Was I not your wife for eight years? Or was I just something added, a decoration like much else here? Is that all our marriage was, for you to collect me and have me on show? Perhaps you forget that I am flesh and blood, I have a mind, a heart, a soul."

"I never thought of you as such," he said sullenly.

"Then why act like this at all? Why bed another woman when your wife needed you by her side the most? I was dying because I lost our son. And I have felt that loss for months and you never talk about it. You didn't fight to say, 'I feel your pain, too, and I miss him'. You swept it away like dust under a rug, like you wanted to forget it ever happened. And when the doctor said that it was not possible for me to birth a child naturally, you went into the arms of someone else, someone who works in our own house. Have you no shame? If it were someone else of a standard of living like ours, I might have accepted it, but to be as low as to hunt among each of the servants, to find someone who might satisfy you—while I was ill and in bed—it is disgusting and base, sir. Shame on you. When I needed you, you were not by my side. Is that my reward, my payment for my love and support when things were sour in your company? If a separation is what you seek, or a divorce, then take it. I prefer the taint of scandal to spending one minute more in this house."

This surprised him. his face went white with shock. Then it changed, flushed a bright pink, blotchy red. His hands clenched into fists. "You don't mean that," he said. "No, I don't believe you mean it."

"I do mean it, sir!" I said with every ounce of passion I could muster, my head lifted in defiance. "I mean every word I have said here tonight. From the very depths of my soul, I mean it. You have used both Mary and I appallingly. Men have done for hundreds of years. Though I know there are good men, decent men out there in the world, they never seem to appear here in the city."

For some strange reason, I mentioned Mr Erisa. What I said about him I can't remember but I know it only drove George into a fury. His face trembled and the vein in is forehead, so prominent and thick, bulged with intensity. There were two seconds when we were silent, then he was on me, his hands folding round my throat, choking me. I don't remember him preparing to lunge for me. One moment he was still, the next he had me against the wall, his hands round my neck and he was choking the life from me. The fierceness in his eyes blazed with intensely and I could not pull mine away. Then he threw me on the floor where I lay squirming. There was no noise, no clamour. No-one would have heard.

Then he loosened his grip, the anger in his eyes softening to shock and horror. Without realizing it, I reached for the poker and struck him on the side of the head. He fell on his side, nursing the wound which leaked through the fingers of his cupped hands. I brought the poker down on his head again when I got up, once, twice, three or four times I hit him and he offered no resistance, gave no cry for me to stop. I thought once again of that wretched woman standing on the gallows waiting to be hanged, and I wondered what she might have said to me:

"You did what you had to. He struck you first. You did what you had to."

When I stopped, he didn't move again. His head was a mass of splintered bone and scarlet blood which glistened in the firelight.

I felt vomit rise in my throat, and I covered my mouth to keep it from coming forth. I looked down at my hands, my gloves were covered in blood. I dropped the poker and it rattled with a clang, the first sound of the night in that room. How could no one have heard what had happened between us? The house must surely be roused.

I pulled my gloves off and threw them into the fire, making sure that no part stuck out and would not be found by the police when they were called. I would not be caught for murder when I was defending myself. *But he softened his grip,* the rational part of my mind told me, the part of my mind that I was not listening to. *He realized what he had done and*

*was going to stop when he saw you were on the ground and his
hands were round your throat.* Then I must come up with a
story which would explain it. I could simply say he would not
let his grip loose. A lie, I know, but how many of us have not
lied when our freedom and lives are in danger?

The fire ate up the gloves completely. I sat on the hearth till
I was sure no fragment was left behind. I had to be sure I
would be safe.

Now, to affect my entrance. I had to make sure the
household noticed me when I came home. I could say that I
had not meant to be late, but I was. I must also have the smell
of drink of my breath, which would let whoever let me in
know I was intoxicated. I splashed some brandy into a glass
and drank thirstily. I already felt the effects of it once the
burning liquid when down my throat.

Down the stairs, quietly, quietly, till I reached the door and
let myself out. I took a step onto the pavement and waited
there a moment. Then an idea struck me. I threw myself onto
the ground and rolled for a little bit. I would say I fell as I was
crossing a road. I had the evidence to prove it on my dress.

I went up the stairs and knocking loudly on the door, loud
enough to rouse the house. I was greeted by Green and Daisy
who, when they saw me, had wide eyes. Daisy wrinkled her
nose for a second to the smell of horse filth on my dress.
Green pulled me inside like a father drawing his naughty
child away from further trouble. I resented him his treatment
of me, but I could not break character now. I must be an actor,
and drunkenness was my role.

"Madam," said Daisy, "oh madam, your lovely dress!"

"I fell," I said meekly, trying my best to look innocent and
upset. I felt like I was back at home with my mother, scolding
me for something trifling she thought most unladylike. Papa
would intervene and tell her to not worry so much. I was a
child, and I deserved to have a little adventure in my life, even

if that meant getting a little dirty now and then. What it was I'd done I can't now remember, but Mama pursed her lips and sent me away to be cleaned and changed. We had guests arriving that evening, and I was expected to make a good impression.

"Take her to her room, Daisy," said Green, and I was led away up the stairs, my arm linked into the crook of Daisy's as we climbed. She did not talk to me, though she treated me with as much delicacy as she could, and when we got to my room she said, "I will help you get out your things, madam. I will have it washed immediately."

"Thank you, Daisy," I said.

I was stripped, and she removed my undergarments. She ran me a bath to get the smell from me, for it had now soaked onto my skin. She would not allow me to let the smell stink the room out or let it seep into my bed linen. I was impatient with their treatment of me; I was a grown woman was I not? I could make these decisions for myself? If I wanted to get more than a little drunk, then I would.

You are living your part, I told myself. *Good. If you keep like this, no-one will suspect the truth.*

The filth on my gown to cover the blood spatters on it, if there were any. The gloves in the fire so they would not be found. I could say I lost them at the Johnsons'. That would work.

When I was put into my nightclothes, Daisy tucked me into bed. She said goodnight. I hesitated for a moment then called her back. "Would you be against the idea of reading to me tomorrow? I know I will feel much better when the headache will come, as it usually does. I am sorry I have caused such a problem tonight." I tried my best to sound genuine.

She smiled and said, "It is no trouble, madam. I am only too happy to help. Yes, I will read to you, if that is what you wish."

"I wish it very much," I said.

She closed the door behind her and I was left alone.

I didn't know what would happen next, and the uncertainty frightened me.

Was I now condemned to spend an eternity in a fiery pit of murderers and adulterers, or would I be let go and allow my crime to consume me and force a confession from me? Would I have a defence for what I did, if I was arrested and taken away? How would I face the taint of scandal when it reared its ugly head? What would I tell the police when they came to examine the body? I would stick to my story, of course. No embellishments. No changes. The only way one is caught is when one fabricates things. If one keeps it simple, then they are sure to get away with whatever they have done.

And in those sleepless hours, I concocted my story. I would keep it small and vague. No point in attaching arms and legs to it when it was fully rounded and needed no explanation. I would keep it running in my mind, and repeated it till I sank into the blissful darkness of sleep.

I do not know how long I slept but I managed to get some rest before I faced the horrors of the new day. I thought about my husband's body in the study, the blood on the floor, the fire dead in its grate, the ash around it. I wondered if any fragments of the gloves I watched burn with eagerness had survived. I prayed there was not. I could not bear it if they had: it would mean I was caught and I was certain to hang.

There was an impatient knock on the door and Green's voice called out to me. "Come," I said, and he entered with a harried look on his face. Sweat beaded his forehead and he started to stammer.

"Madam," he said, "I don't know how to put this delicately. I fear there is no way I can. We went to the study this morning, madam, and Mr Campbell was inside."

"Had he been there all night?" I asked.

"That is what's wrong, madam. Mr Campbell has been murdered. He's dead in his study. I ought to call the police, but I did not want to do so without telling you, madam."

The colour drained from my face. I was no longer acting. I did not imagine it would be so quick before he was found, and the investigations of the police would come to harass me for the truth. I felt the sickness rise in me, climbing my throat with insidious slowness. It would be some time before it came, but I knew it would soon. I held on to my composure and said, "Find the police. Summon a constable."

"Yes madam," he said and left me.

I sat up stupefied. The story I told myself throughout the night had vanished suddenly.

Fear struck me. I remembered reading a strange story by an American poet, a gruesome story about a young man who had never hated the man he killed, but had done so due to his having "the evil eye", and was discovered because he confessed the deed, the hammering of a heart under the floorboards having driven him mad at last with remorse.

I would not allow myself to be driven to such extremes. I was not in a story; my freedom depended on what I was to say and do now.

I got out of bed, sober and heavy. I rang for Daisy who arrived full of tears. "Oh madam," she said when she saw me. She threw herself into my arms like a daughter seeking the protection of her mother. I hushed and comforted her as best I could and dried her tears.

"Do not worry, darling, there is nothing to be afraid of. The police are on their way and they will discover the killer. You have nothing to fear."

"But madam, there is something I have to tell you," she said, but I cut her off.

"Hush now; we can discuss it later. I am sure it is not so important as you think. Come, help me get dressed."

She did so in silence, but her hands trembled. She was nervous, I could see; I could not hold it against her, for I was just as nervous, if not more so. The police were coming to find me and would do their best to ensure I—or the person they thought did it—was caught. Finally, I was decently clothed and stepped out of my room with Daisy on my arm. The whole house was filled with persons and voices, some hurried, others took their time. I looked over the bannister to see a funny little man with cat-like movements and narrowed eyes look around then turn them up at me.

My body froze. I recognized him, but could not recall from where. Our eyes held each other's gaze for some time before he said, "Mrs Campbell?" His voice was thick with an accent I couldn't place. Was it Irish or Scotch?

I nodded and said, "I am she, yes."

"Very good. I will speak to you in a few moments, Mrs Campbell; is there anywhere in the house you might make yourself comfortable?"

"We shall be in the drawing room, sir," I said.

He nodded and went on talking with a subordinate of his.

We waited in the drawing room for fifteen minutes before the gentleman came to speak with us. He gave a polite knock and when I called for him to enter, he did so with meekness, a kind of gentility I had never known in any man I had ever met. Green trailed in after him and announced him as Inspector Black. He bowed to us and I bowed my head in response. Inspector Black turned his eye over the room and gave a sigh of satisfaction.

"Forgive me," he said, "I do admire these kinds of houses. Such fine art goes into their making, even on plain things such as doors. The brass knob, you observe, the man who forged it put a great deal love into doing so. It is a pity that such manufacture is not appreciated as it ought to be."

He fell silent for a moment, then shook his head as if ridding it of the thought he was following. He asked if he was permitted to sit on the sofa opposite. I said he most welcome to.

When he had settled himself, he clasped his hands together, leaning back in the chair, a little too comfortably for my liking, and said, "You will pardon my presence here; I understand it must be very distressing for you, Mrs Campbell. I can only extend my deepest sympathies to you in this difficult time." He tried his best to offer a smile which would be of comfort, then he said, "Am I to understand you have not yet seen your husband's body?"

I shook my head. "No, I have not." Deep down, the question affronted me. As I feared, my reaction was to be gauged. If I did not master my emotions, I would be found out.

"For the better, I think," he said.

I asked him a question that struck my ear as odd, but I thought it would be better doing so. "How did he die?"

Inspector Black was taken aback somewhat. I had an inkling he would turn to using the tack of it was not right for a lady of my standing to know the details of such things. I cut in.

"When I was a girl, I watched a young woman hanged for murder. It is an image which haunts me daily. My father tried to protect me from the cruelty of the world. He tried his best and it was not enough. So, you will excuse me if I say I have the stomach for such details. Now please, tell me how my husband died."

He was reluctant to tell me, I know; but he went through the details. He had been hit on the head with a hard instrument, and whoever hit him did not stop at one. His skull was cracked and bone was exposed. He must have died in great pain, he said.

Daisy's hand tightly grasped my own; I felt her shudder. I had a notion she was going to be violently sick.

I felt it rise in me too, though I mastered myself in time.

We recovered together. She is a strong girl, and the colour was back in her cheeks in a few moments.

"I am sorry to have distressed your companion so," said Inspector Black. "I did not think it right to tell, but you did ask it of me."

"I would prefer to know now than find out at the inquest or the trial, should it come to that. Have you any leads? Do you know if it was a man or a woman?"

"Not any yet, but some things have been found. And we have an idea as to who might have done it."

I felt my stomach turn to ice, but I kept my composure. "I see," I said.

Silence passed between us, then Inspector Black said that he had a few questions for me to answer. They were the usual questions, he assured me, nothing pointed, nothing assumed.

Where were you last night? "At a party, at the Johnsons' house. I was there for a while, I drank some wine, I chatted with some friends. I believe I made a bit of a spectacle of myself on my way home. I had a little too much to drink. I was quite all right when I was leaving. It was not until I was walking home that I started to feel the effects of it."

What time did you come home last night? "I couldn't tell you I am afraid. The servants might know. Daisy and Mr Green were the ones who let me in."

Black turned to them and they said I came home at about three-thirty in the morning.

Do you know if your husband had enemies? "He was a businessman; I thought enemies were an everyday hazard."

"Not the kind that murder," said Inspector Black.

I nodded. Silence passed between us again then he went on.

Did you notice anything strange about your husband's behaviour of late?

Did I notice he was having an affair with a parlour maid, that he was thinking of asking for a separation or divorce?

"No, nothing I could detect as strange. He was curiously lacking in emotion when it was a matter of business. He did not confide to me any of his woes, if there were any."

Do you think it was a rival that killed your husband? "It is entirely possible; however, I know nothing worth killing over in the company or its competitiveness. It was a simple business of stationery. I am sure my husband would have been sent threats from other manufacturers, a usual thing, I would imagine; not so novel as one would expect. I always thought they might be a spiteful kind of joke in order to get my husband to be anxious and deterred to do any business further."

The detective gave me a measuring look and stroked his chin.

"This is very true. It is not so novel as one might think. Businessmen receive all manner of unpleasant letters through the post. And you say there were no troubles between you both?"

"As I said, I wouldn't know, Inspector. My husband and I were not on confiding terms and I, as most men would attest, as a woman would not have the head for business."

He blushed a little trying to smile humorously.

"Thank you, Mrs Campbell. You have been very helpful."

He rose to his feet and turned to leave then stopped and said, "Ah!" turning back to us. "There was one more thing, I just remembered." He wasn't facing me, but directing his talk to Daisy who sat trembling at my side. "I had it told me that you, Miss Daisy, went to see the master of the house about something. What was it about?"

My heart hammered. Daisy went to see him? Panic bubbled inside me and I wanted to deflect the whole thing from her. As a daughter she was to me, and I would defend her thus. I thought, *Now is the time! Tell him the truth before he makes the wrong arrest!* But I didn't. I was silent the whole time. If I confessed, it might be that the answer was trivial; I would reveal the truth and condemn myself. I managed to control the tumult within and listen to what she had to say.

Daisy was shaking now, unable to keep still she clutched my hand in both hers. It hurt. She started to cry now and turned to me and she said in a panic, "Oh madam, madam, I won't go to prison, will I? I won't be hanged?"

The panic was enough to rend a heart of stone. How could she, a child so innocent and good think she would be hanged for something she didn't do? But whatever it was, I needed to know. I would not let her take the blame for something I had done, if that is where it was going to lead.

"Of course not," I said. "Just answer the question, child. You are in no danger."

"Definitely not," said Black. "I merely wished to ask what was the nature of your visit."

She glanced at me then at the inspector and said, "There were two reasons why I went to him. The first was about a girl in the house. Mary's her name. She's been high and mighty of late and I went to ask him about what we were to do. Most of the staff wanted to leave because she—" she stopped and looked at me, the tears in her eyes returned "Oh madam, I'm sorry but I must speak the truth."

"Then speak it," I said.

"Mary had been having some kind of connection with Mr Campbell. The whole house knew it but they didn't dare say anything. We were too afraid we'd lose our jobs, and she loved it. She loved this hold she had over us. It was Mary's day off yesterday, but she was in the room that night, before I went to see him. She was frightfully angry about something. I heard them at it, shouting. She was the one shouting mainly, but I heard Mr Campbell's voice say something I couldn't catch. Then Mary said, 'I'll kill you, I swear to God, if you do this, I will kill you!' The door burst open and Mary came out with a face like thunder. She spotted me and snapped that if I were to stand there and stare, then she'd have my guts out, too, such were her words. I have never been so frightened of someone in my life."

"Did she come back? Do you know?"

"No, sir," she said, shaking her head. "I don't. It's more than possible she did, and quietly did it. We heard nothing. That's why it was such a shock to us. We heard nothing. None of the servants did."

"It is a big house," I said, "and the servants live below. It is natural that you would hear nothing, dearest."

"Yes, madam," she said at last, relaxing slightly.

"Aye, this is a perfect explanation," said Black. "Now, would you mind telling us the second reason?"

Daisy's face coloured. "No, of course not. I went to see him because I needed help. There has been a complication with my family and I needed to take the time away from the house. My old father is not long for this earth. I could not say anything to you, madam, as you were heading out, and I only received the letter when you were at your party. I needed to see someone in charge and ask for the time away I needed to be there when he goes. I was going to tell you as soon as I could, madam, I swear I was."

I went back to soothing her and held her in my arms like a mother comforting her child. "There is nothing to worry about, of course you can go to see your father. Where does he stay? I can have him brought here, if you wish, and it will be more convenient for the doctor to come and see how he is doing. I will pay the expenses."

Daisy burst into tears when I told her I would pay for it. I paid her a good sum as my lady's maid, but I knew that that sum would be eaten by the doctor's bills when they came. And the costs of funerals would be astronomical. I would not see my girl's father put in a pauper's grave so I said I would pay for that too, when the time came.

"Thank you, madam," she said through her tears. "Thank you!"

The door burst open and with the dramatics of a stage play, Mary appeared in the room and pointed a short, stumpy finger at me. "Murderess! Murderess" she cried. "Arrest her!"

Black got to his feet and slowly turned to her. "What's this?"

"You heard me, are you deaf? She killed him, arrest her at once!"

For a moment there was utter silence; then Black took the stage and said with a voice as hard as rock, "You have a nerve, my girl, to come bursting in here and accusing your employer of murder. You realize that is slander, and there is a law against that. You will go to a nasty little prison for a very long time, my girl. You know that, don't you?"

"It is not slander if it is the truth," she said, her head raised in defiance. "And all I know is that she killed my lover."

"Ah yes. You must be Mary."

"I am she. And I know that *that* woman is a murderess, and I demand you arrest her at once!"

"That's some awfully strong language for a maid to be taking against her employer, and if your accusation is false—"

"It is *not* false!" she screamed. "I know I am right."

"This letter will prove otherwise," said Black, pulling from his coat pocket a folded paper and opening it read:

Dear Mary—You must forgive me writing you this letter, and I wish there was a way to do this better than has been done. It is not fair to you, or fair to my wife, that I have used you thus. She knows how badly I have treated her, and I have placed you higher than her. That now must come to an end, as sad as it is to write those words. It has been a great help to me and I am very grateful. I love you

155

very much but I must think now of my wife and the future. I hope you will one day forgive me for all I have done to you, just as I pray she will forgive me. I plan to speak to her on (date omitted) and we will live as we ought to. I must also ask you to look for a new position in another house. I will write for you a good reference, you can count on that. And I intend to settle on you an allowance of £100 a year. I hope this will be enough.

Kindest regards and yours with regret,

George Campbell

I felt the sting of tears behind my eyes. At once I shook and fainted.

When I woke, I found myself in my room, having been carried there by two policemen and I was being looked after by Daisy. I heard in the distance a voice familiar and unwanted. I heard Agatha in the hallway, admonishing someone.

Oh God, not Agatha.

"Daisy," I said weakly. "A glass of water, please."

As though by magic she produce a glass from the table and pressed it against my lips. It was cool and refreshing. "What happened," I started then Green cut in.

"Mary has been taken away. She has been arrested. The letter was enough to make her break."

"She confessed?" I asked.

"No, but there is no way she can deny it."

I lay there with wide eyes. The world did not seem real, and I was somehow caught in a dream. Everything was blurry, but the sounds around me were distinct.

"I took the liberty of sending for Mrs Griffiths. I know it was not my place, but I thought you could use someone close and dear in this difficult time."

"Thank you, Green," I said. "That was very kind of you."

I tried to sit up. Green helped and propped me against the pillows. "A doctor is on the way, madam," he said. "But Inspector Black would like a word with you, when you are feeling better."

"I am better now," I said. "Please send him in."

Green turned and opened the door. It was not Black that came in first but Agatha, and wailing like a phantom hurled herself towards me and knelt by the bedside, embracing me.

"Darling," she said through her tears. "Are you all right? This whole wretched business is simply too much for you, it must be. We have made arrangements. You will come with us for a few days, and we will go away."

"I can't do that," I said. "There is the inquest to attend—"

"Hang the inquest, they have the girl! The little monster will pay for what she did."

Black stood in the doorway. Our eyes met and I said at last, "Agatha, I must speak with the inspector alone. Please, would you mind?"

She was reluctant to leave but she did so without argument. She closed the door behind her.

Alone with the inspector was not so intimidating as I thought it would be. We smiled, he said he admired this room out of all he had been in, then coloured when he realized what he was saying.

"Mrs Campbell, I must ask you to be very honest with me. Did you know your husband was having an affair?"

There was no point hiding now. He knew the truth of Mary and my husband. I thought, *Has he known throughout our entire interview that my husband was unfaithful?*

"Yes," I said. "I knew he was having an affair."

"And you did not dismiss her for this?"

"What would be the point, sir? Other than to cause more misery and heartache which was strong enough in this house.

I am a grown woman. I know when a man no longer needs a wife to love him and needs a whore to pleasure."

"I heard you had recovered from an illness. Had it anything to do with that?"

"I suppose it had," I said. "I don't know any more. He told me it started when I lay on the sickbed. He didn't know where to direct his urges, so I suppose he wanted a mistress to take on my role when I was not there. I don't know why. What woman ever knows why her husband does the things he does? But he did it. Of course, I was not happy about it. But I wouldn't kill him for it. So many marriages have mistresses and lovers attached, and they know about it all. Why should mine be any different? Was he a born philanderer? Perhaps. Was he afraid of losing me? I don't know. We never discussed it. But I would not kill him because of it."

"Then what would you have done?"

Here it was: the question for all women in these situations. *What would you have done?*

"I would have left this house and taken residence somewhere away from the city. I would allow the affair to continue, but I would not wish to be under the same roof when it was going on. Divorce is useless to us, sir. I must find ten counts of infidelity whereas my husband only needs two or three. Divorce is always in favour of the husband. A woman is tainted, fallen. We greatly fear scandal. The man is praised as the rightful party, though his methods are frowned on. And when he moved on, he would find someone else, use her up and go on to the next.

"You see, inspector, we women must bear it, as my friend Mrs Griffiths says. And she is right. What we do for our men is far greater than what our men do for us. We keep their homes, we make them feel comfortable, we bring up their children. And we are given abuse for it all when we asked for fidelity. The men I have known, and there are men I know, who think that it is natural for a man to seek a mistress, that they are ruled by their desires. Then I ask, sir, why the sudden contradiction. Are not we women ruled by their desires and emotions? Or is that an excuse you have made so you can take any woman you please? My husband's sin was that he had no self-control. He had no way to kerb his urges and so they overcame him. I know not if he has had many mistresses or if Mary was the first."

Black was silent; he did not interrupt the flow of my words, nor did he contradict them as another man might. He did not defend his sex as most other men would. He knew the pain I had experienced. I could see it in his eyes. Was he remembering something from his own life which had rattled his core and squeezed his heart? Had he seen mother entertain another man or had he seen his father with another woman? I was surprised by his sensitivity.

"You are right," he said. "We men often cannot control ourselves; and it is not a matter of our gender, but our actions. Our nature we cannot control. Like the scorpion and the toad. A scorpion cannot control his nature, but he can control his actions, can he not?"

"I am familiar with the story," I said.

"Not many I know are. But I have come across a case like this, oh, some years ago now. A wife who had killed her husband. But it was different. She killed him in self-defence. I did my duty, as must we all, but I did not want her to be hanged."

"She confessed, did she not?"

"Yes," said Black. "She did. Beat her husband's head in with a rolling pin."

"You investigated, and were sympathetic?"

"Entirely. But when the court took it, it was out of my hands."

"She was the woman I saw hang, sir."

We were silent for a few moments more. The air between us crackled. In this room were two murderers. One who did his duty, the other to defend herself. He turned and made for the door as he begged leave. There was a guarantee that Mary would be sent to trial and hanged. I nodded and said that as long as justice was done, I had no quarrel with it. He nodded and went to the door.

"Oh yes, once again I forgot. Your lady's maid said that you had a fall in the night? Am I right in saying so?"

"Yes, I had."

"And the dress you wore was rather ruined. I saw when I talked to the servants. What a lovely gown. Just as lovely as the cloak hanging on the peg by the door. Quite a fortunate thing, then, that that hadn't been spoiled, too."

He turned and left the room.

Melt not in weeping
while she lies sleeping

Melt not in weeping
while she lies sleeping

Deep in the forest where no people go stands a wall of thorns for which no man or woman can give reason. Witches have tried to kill it by poisoning its roots; wizards have tried by magic to burn it down, to little success. No one knows its purpose, or where it came from. There are no visible entries; anyone who tries to get in never comes back.

But a traveller came one day and found a way in and came back too, though no-one believed him afterwards.

It was a day of winter and snow had fallen in the night. Trees jutted out of the white blanket blackened as though burned with cold, their naked limbs shivering in the breeze that passed through. Our traveller walked along the path with horse in tow. It pulled a cart filled with linen he was to sell in the City, where he knew he would earn enough to buy a gift, a gift that would change the way people looked at him. He wanted to find a present for a girl in his village; but he was poor and his father would not lend him the money to find a gift suitable for her, and there was already a suitor in her sights, one who had more to give than he, our traveller.

But he sought to win her heart through her love, by his passion than by a coin-heavy purse.

Snow crunched under his boots; the horse ambled peaceably by his side.

Then the horse took fright, reared and whinnied; its forelegs punched the air. The traveller calmed him and soothed him, patting his neck and speaking words of comfort. He could not see anything that could have startled him thus, but he did feel something was very wrong.

They rounded a corner and it stood before them: prickly, tall, lethal.

The wall of thorns, the forest to which entry was forbidden, was silent as an open grave. Smoke reached out from between the trunks and horny branches. The horse whinnied again but did not rear. Our traveller felt his friend's panic in himself but would not show it.

"Come now," he said soothingly. "There is nothing to be afraid of. I will show you."

The animal, who loved and trusted his master, waited patiently for his friend to show him. The traveller went to the wall and placed a hand on one of the great horny boughs.

He turned and smiled when the bough gave way.

Our traveller went tumbling in.

The horse gave another frightened scream and reared. The traveller could hear his frantic thrashing. He feared the horse would hurt himself if the cart overturned and the wood splintered. He called out: "Nothing is wrong, I just fell." The horse calmed at once.

He was about to step out when he looked around and saw a little way off a small thatch-roofed house.

A cottage, much like the one in which he lived with his family.

Now this was awfully peculiar, and the sight of it made him uneasy. He had never heard tell of a house here, and if he had, it was from stories and fairy tales, like that of the maiden with the red cloak who ran to granny's house and was greeted by a wolf.

He walked, slowly, trying to avoid contact with the long thorns that jutted from every direction: left, right, above and below. One spike came close to poking his groin, which he narrowly avoided. As he got closer, he noticed the air became cooler and cleaner. It felt fresh, crisper than he had ever known winter air to be, and there was warmth in the breeze.

Nearing the edge of the thorny forest, he saw no snow beyond.

There was a garden full of flowers. Green grass, and butter-flies flitted this way and that. Roses, hollyhocks, geraniums, primroses, all grew beside one another. Ivy climbed a frame on the left cheek of the house.

There was woman on her hands and knees, planting a flower in the ground.

The traveller tumbled out the woods, fell, then hastily got to his feet.

The woman did not flinch, even when he cleared his throat. She did not answer though she knew he was there.

She went on planting her flower.

"You've come at a very strange time," she said at last. "I didn't expect anyone to come, not this time of year."

She got to her feet and turned to face him. She was an old crone with a gentle face, the lines about her mouth and cheeks that of laughter and smiles.

Her green eyes twinkled merrily behind wire spectacles.

"I expect you've come to see her," she said. "Come, come!" she grabbed his wrist and yanked him inside. The cottage was small but comfortable: chairs ready and a plate of cookies and cakes sat on the table between them. The old woman was expecting company.

"Sit down, I'll make a pot of tea."

The traveller obediently sat on a plush armchair before a crackling fire. The warmth was welcome to his nipping fingers.

She came back with two cups held on saucers—cute little bone china things with painted flowers.

One of them had a chip on the rim.

"Like I said," the old woman said when she too sat down, "I wasn't expecting anyone to appear. Not today. There's been plenty peoples coming and going. Usually they forget where they've been after they've gone. They've all come to find out what's beyond the wall of thorns. But not you," she added pointedly.

The traveller blushed, put his cup on the table, and spoke in a flustered way.

"Well," he said, "I have always been curious."

"And curiosity's no sin," said the old woman. "Yet you've never sought what lies beyond that wall. What brought you here?"

"An accident, I assure you." He gave the account of his horse taking fright and how he sought to calm him. The old woman smiled and gave a little chuckle.

"Very sweet you are to your animals," she said. "More like you needed in this world."

He flushed a bright red and took a sip from his cup of tea. It was delicious stuff; he felt life and strength seep back into his limbs which no longer ached with cold.

"I suppose you'll want to see her," said the old woman, mentioning again this "her" of whom he had no knowledge. "You'll want to know who she is, won't you?" The traveller said nothing; he couldn't find the words to speak. "Don't fret," she went on, "don't fret, you'll learn soon enough. You'll learn."

She got to her feet and grabbed his wrist again. He put the cup and saucer down. It landed with a clatter. He hoped he hadn't broken it or spilled its contents. The old crone took him to a flight of stairs and up they went; slowly, very slowly, they came to a door and she put her finger to her lips. She opened it a crack and peered inside.

"All clear," she said. They went in, then our traveller saw her.

On a bed, made comfortable with plump pillows beneath the web of golden-red hair, her face delicate and shimmering in a shaft of light that streamed from the window, was a girl, about the same age as our traveller. Beautiful she was, with clear skin and red lips.

She did not stir when they entered, and the old woman went about on tiptoe as to not disturb her, she sat on a low stool by the bed. The girl's hands were rested on top of one another, beneath them, clasped to her chest, was a red rose.

The traveller gasped softly. He had never seen so beautiful a creature in all his life; even the girl from his village of whom he was enamoured could not compare. So gentle was she, so fair, light radiating from her in that stream of white.

"No movement," said the old woman. "Not that there would be. No matter how hard I try." She drew a pin from her pocket, took the girl's hand in her own, straightened a finger, and pressed the sharp point into the girl's skin. The traveller stepped forward to stop her but the girl did not wake. There was little blood.

"See," said the crone. "No movement. She won't wake. The spell's too strong. And no matter what I do, she'll never look on me again."

The traveller stood trembling.

"Who is she?"

"In life," said the crone, "she was a girl like any other girl, though she was the daughter of a king and queen. So, I suppose you'd call her a princess. She was the sweetest, kindest, fairest girl in the world and everyone said so. I didn't stand a chance against her sweetness when she came to me. I was young then, and had my own beauty to speak of; and she came to me full of life, with the brightest smile I'd ever seen. I loved her from that moment on. And I hope to God she knew it. Even if I don't know if she loved me back."

The crone sighed the trembling sigh of one on the verge of tears.

"She fell ill one day. No-one knew how or why. It just happened. She fell asleep another day and never woke again. We found on her finger a small bead of blood. She'd pricked it on a rose somewhere."

The traveller listened and watched the girl as she slept; the gentle rise and fall of her chest as she breathed, the delicate way the crone replaced her ward's hand on her chest, having wrapped a piece of torn cloth round the pricked finger. "She did not wake—not when the apothecaries came, not when the fairies came to cast their spells, not even when her mother and father sat by her bed every night, weeping, hoping she'd come back. She sleeps on, and her face never changes. She never ages, never feels pain, never withers, never dies. But the things around her do." She turned to the traveller forlornly and something of a smile crept across her lips. "I will die soon. Only a matter of time, as these things are. But I will not complain. I've had a good life. I've done my duty to her, as she would have me do."

The traveller said nothing; he went on staring at the girl. Not dead. Only sleeping.

Like the story of Arthur, for he is not dead, merely at rest. And he will rise again like the God Christ from his resting place. One day.

For this girl it had been years, decades.

"Kiss her," said the old crone. The traveller was astonished. "Kiss her, just once, on the lips. A peck. She'd like that. She used to kiss the people she liked. You're the first she's had in a long time. None of the others would kiss her. They only wanted to claim her when she woke up. My lady is not to be claimed. She's mine. Mine and mine alone."

The old crone suddenly changed, became defensive. She struggled to rise to her feet but did so after a few attempts. She stared with wild eyes at our traveller, then seemed to recover herself. There was no apology.

He approached the bed, bent himself low and pressed his lips against the sleeping girl's.

She was warm, and when his lips touched hers there was a tingling sensation, a crackle of magic he had never experienced.

For a moment he stared, wondering what change might occur if he waited. Would it make her rise and open her eyes? Would she stretch out her arms and yawn? Would she giggle when she saw she had company? Would she would greet him graciously and ask if he would stay to dinner?

The sleeping girl did not move.

The crone must have thought she would awake, too, for she was now very tense as she watched him get close, she even gasped. But when she saw there was nothing, she loosened and let her shoulders slump; her head dipped forward resting her chin on her chest.

"There now," said she. "You've seen enough."

She ushered him out of the room and down the stairs.

"It's time you were getting back to your horse, was it not?"

The traveller did not respond, but gathered his things and made for the door. The old woman followed. Out in the garden where the flowers grew the first flakes of snow started to fall. The air was cold and the butterflies fell to the ground in sweet, sad spirals.

The old woman sighed her deep, trembling sigh, but for the traveller she had a smile.

"On your way now, the path will be clear," she said.

Taking his arm, she made him lean down and, to his astonishment, she planted a kiss on his cheek.

"Thank you for coming," she said. "You made her very happy."

The traveller smiled ruefully and turned for the thorny forest. When he looked back, he saw the old woman smiling still with her eyes full of tears. She waved to him. A little more into the woods, he turned again. The old woman was gone. The house was a ruin, like it had not been lived in for a hundred years or more, crumbling and grey. But flowers and ivy still grew about, wrapping their eager tendrils round it, ready to swallow it.

He went on through the thorns and told himself he would not look back.

When he got to the other side his horse stood waiting. Upon seeing him the beast was overjoyed and hurried over to nuzzle his master's face. After a while, the traveller looked back to the forest of thorn.

It had vanished. Only a snow-covered clearing faced him. Trees surrounded it, and a stream of light filtered through the bare boughs like a light from heaven.

In the middle of that pool of light lay a strange mark imprinted in the snow, like someone had left a large shape there. Before his eyes the indent began to fill, and he noticed, as he watched, a second form appear, the shape of a sleeping girl. Her hands were clasped over her chest, a rose lay underneath; her eyes were closed. Her hair spread like a web of ice.

Then the girl of snow opened her eyes, turned to the traveller and smiled. She lifted a hand from her chest and blew him a kiss goodbye. She melted away in seconds.

On the ground a rose was left, the petals turning crimson as if they bled.

With tears, he took his prize and turned for home.

Short story collections available from Evertype

The Scarlet Petal and other stories
(Ryan Petrie 2021)

The Mighty Woman's Adventures Abroad
(Art de Creag, tr. Mícheál Ó hAodha 2020)

Letter from my Foster Mother and other stories
(Fionntán de Brún, tr. Mícheál Ó hAodha 2020)

The Book of Poison (Panu Petteri Höglund & S. Albert Kivinen,
tr. Colin Parmer & Tino Warinowski 2014)

The Partisan and other Stories (Gabriel Rosenstock,
tr. Mícheál Ó hAodha & Gabriel Rosenstock 2014)

A Nosegay of Pleasant Delights: Five-minute fictions (Brian S. Lee 2012)

The Burning Woman and other stories (Frank Roger 2012)

*Neighbours: Stories in Mennonite Low German and English
Nohbasch: Jeschichte opp Plautdietsch enn Enjlisch*
(Jack Thiessen 2014)

*Nosy Neighbours: Stories in Mennonite Low German and English
Nieschieaje Nohbasch: Jeschichte opp Plautdietsch enn Enjlisch*
(Jack Thiessen 2015)